Derrick Widmer

# POST-SOVIET RUSSIA IN THE ADVENTUROUS 1990'S – THE WILD DECADE
Privatization, Oligarchs, Mafia and Vodka

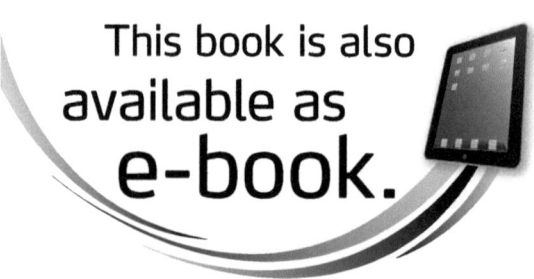

www.novumpublishing.com

All rights of distribution, including via film, radio, and television, photomechanical reproduction, audio storage media, electronic data storage media, and the reprinting of portions of text, are reserved.

Printed in the European Union on eco-friendly, chlorine-free and acid-free bleached paper.

© 2019 novum publishing

ISBN 978-3-99064-670-0
Translated from German into English by Elizabeth H. Schneewind
Cover photos: Derrick Widmer; Alexey Fedorov | Dreamstime.com
Cover design, layout & typesetting: novum publishing
Internal illustrations: see bibliography p.10

The images provided by the author have been printed in the highest possible quality.

**www.novumpublishing.com**

"Life can only be *understood* by looking backwards,
But it must be *lived* by looking forwards"

(Sören Kierkegaard 1813–1855,
Danish philosopher, writer)

## Inhaltsverzeichnis

Chapter 1 .................................... 15
FROM RUSSIA WITH LOVE

Chapter 2 .................................... 22
THE ADVENTURE BEGINS IN MOSCOW

Chapter 3 .................................... 34
THE END OF THE SOVIET UNION 1991

Chapter 4 .................................... 37
PRIVATIZATION – A SYSTEM BUILT
ON VOUCHERS AND AUCTIONS – 1992 TO 1994

Chapter 5 .................................... 44
OUR SECOND TIME IN MOSCOW – SEPTEMBER 1993

Chapter 6 .................................... 52
OMINOUS TENSION FILLS THE AIR

Chapter 7 .................................... 57
THE CRISIS IS PAST – REMINISCENCES

Chapter 8 .................................... 64
ON-SITE EVALUATION OF VARIOUS CEMENT
WORKS – IMPLEMENTING THE CONCEPT OF
"DUE DILIGENCE" – NOVEMBER–DECEMBER 1993

Chapter 9 .................................... 72
POVERTY AND INFLATION IN RUSSIA

Chapter 10 .................................... 75
APPLICATION TO THE HOLDERBANK EXECUTIVE
COMMITEE FOR A MANDATE TO NEGOTIATE
A PARTNERSHIP WITH ALFA CEMENT –
DECEMBER, 1993

Chapter 11 .................................... 78
FROM MOSCOW TO PERM AND THEN ON TO
GORNOSAVODSK – JANUARY, 1994

Chapter 12 .................................... 86
THE CONTRACT WITH ALFA CEMENT:
FROM A ROUGH DRAFT TO A FINALIZED DEAL,
READY FOR SIGNING – JANUARY TO MAY 1994

Chapter 13 .................................... 90
A RETURN TO THE BONE-CHILLING CLIMATE OF
THE URALS – (AND HOW THIS HARSH CLIMATE
HAD INFLUENCED HISTORY) –
FEBRUARY & MARCH 1994

Chapter 14 .................................... 95
"HOLDERBANK" – BODYGUARDS and a RENTED
STRETCH-LIMOUSINE – 1994

Chapter 15 .................................... 97
SADKO – THE FIRST LUXURY SHOPPING CENTER
IN MOSCOW – (THREATENED AT THE OUTSET BY
MAFIA EXTORTION)

Chapter 16 .................................... 99
TOUGH NEGOTIATIONS

Chapter 17 .................................... 101
THE CONTRACT BETWEEN HOLDERBANK
AND ALFA CEMENT – MAY 1994

Chapter 18 .................................... 103
PRIVATIZATION AND PLEDGE AUCTIONS
(LOANS FOR SHARES) – 1995 TO 1999

Chapter 19 .................................... 106
THE RISE OF THE OLIGARCHS – 1995 TO 1997

Chapter 20 .................................... 113
A FIRST VISIT TO SHUROVO (SHUROVSKY
TSEMENT) – MARCH/APRIL, 1994

Chapter 21 .................................... 118
IN THE FAR EAST OF RUSSIA: SPASSK –
NOVEMBER 5–11, 1994

Chapter 22 .................................... 130
TRAVELING FURTHER FROM SPASSK TO
NAKHODKA AND THEN TO VLADIVOSTOK –
NOVEMBER 1994

Chapter 23 .................................... 135
ENTER THE WORLD BANK (IFC) NEGOTIATIONS
FROM AUTUMN 1994 TO WINTER 1995–96

Chapter 24 .................................... 138
BY PRIVATE PLANE FROM MOSCOW TO PERM –
SEPTEMBER 1995

Chapter 25 .................................... 144
MOSCOW-KOLUMNA, MOSCOW-PERM –
MARCH 20–23, 1996

Chapter 26 .................................... 149
ORGANIZATIONAL AND FINANCIAL
CONSOLIDATION PHASE OF ALFA CEMENT – 1994–96

Chapter 27 .................................. 151
ARTISTIC EXPERIENCES DURING OUR TIME IN
RUSSIA – 1993–1998

Chapter 28 .................................. 158
ALFA CEMENT JOINS THE HOLDERBANK GROUP –
1996–1999

Chapter 29 .................................. 167
THE YEARS 1998 TO 2000

Chapter 30 .................................. 175
THE FINANCIAL CRISIS – 1998

Chapter 31 .................................. 177
CONSOLIDATION OF THE RUSSIAN CEMENT
INDUSTRY – 1994–2011

Chapter 32 .................................. 181
RUSSIA TODAY AND TOMORROW

Chapter 33 .................................. 189
CONCLUSION

Chapter 34 .................................. 191
ACKNOWLEDGMENTS

**Copyrights:**
p. 33, 62, 63, 84, 85, 102, 117, 128, 134, 142, 147, 148, 180 © Derrick Widmer,
p. 54 © KEYSTONE/AP Photo/Alexander Zemlianchenko,
p. 12, 13 © ID 72449278 © Stan Parkh | Dreamstime.com

## Chapter 1

## FROM RUSSIA WITH LOVE

In the beginning of 1993, during my absence abroad, a man named Michael Alexandrov appeared at the cement group Holderbank, later called Holcim. He asked to have a discussion with the director about investment possibilities in the Russian cement industry. At the beginning of privatization, this Russian had acquired, together with a group of Russian cement managers, a number of vouchers (financial participations) in various Russian cement works. Mr. Alexandrov was looking for a global industrial partner for increased development of cement interests in Russia. As no one in Holderbank was interested or had time for this matter, it landed eventually with my very agile and clever assistant, Dominik Wlodarczak.

Like me, he was very interested in the political and economic upheaval in Russia. After all, it had been little more than a year since, on December 1, 1991, to everyone's surprise, the red flag with the hammer and sickle was taken down from the cupola of the Kremlin in Moscow. The Soviet Union finally ceased to exist.

Let us go back a few years.

From the time of the First World War, the Russian imperium was of vast dimensions and included as well the greater part of Poland and all of Finland.

From 1917 until 1941 the Soviet Union (USSR) was a single state of incredible geographical dimensions, presenting a dramatic experiment in its political and economic systems. The economy was based on state ownership of all means of production.

All planning was done by the state, as were all production goals and agricultural goals. Between the twenties and the fifties the Soviet Union achieved, with rapid economic growth, the construction of an impressive, almost frighteningly large economic and military power.

The war against the German aggressor (1941–1945) was described as the "Great War for the Fatherland," a reference to the 1812 "War for the Fatherland" against Napoleon Bonaparte. Fourteen million Red soldiers died in the Second World War. At the beginning the Soviet Union had a very large army, with in part very modern equipment. It had by any measure the greatest army of tanks in the world, a great number of guns and airplanes, and a very large and well-equipped infantry (20,000 tanks, 17,000 airplanes, 34,000 guns, and 5.7 million soldiers)! In 1950 the Soviet army was numerically the strongest army in the world. The Soviet Union strove with all its might to maintain parity with the USA in the arms race.

The Cold War, which lasted from 1945 to 1990, divided the world into two hostile blocs. Throughout these decades almost everyone in the free world saw this as a constant threat, leading both east and west to arming and to a demonstration of military might as had never been seen before. It was, after all, the declared goal of the Soviet Union to command universal power. And various dangerous undertakings showed that it was quite serious in its goals and would not hold back in a military conflict with the west bloc: The Berlin blockade and the American airlift in 1948 to 1949; the march on Hungary with Soviet tanks in 1956; the building of the Berlin wall, forty-three kilometers long of concrete and barbed wire, in 1961 and remaining in place until 1989; the Cuban missile crisis in 1963, with the threat of an atomic war; and the march on Czechoslovakia in 1968, putting brutally to an end the Prague Spring, a period of political liberalization in Czechoslovakia. In 1953 the USSR exploded the first hydrogen bomb and developed intercontinental ballistic missiles. The Soviets also demonstrated military and technical competence with the first Sputnik (satellite program 1957). In 15 years they wanted to gain equality with and surpass the USA. After the USSR demonstrated their mastery in a shocking way with the Sputnik flight on October 4, 1957, they demonstrated again with their Voshod program for manned missiles a superiority in racing and their superior mastery in everything else. On Feb. 21, 1962, Yuri Gagarin circulated the earth in 108 minutes in his Vostok-3 capsule. He became the first USSR pop-star and was the most famous person of the year (Neue Zurcher Zeitung (NZZ), April 2011). As reaction President John F. Kennedy declared on May 25, 1962, in a special joint session of Congress:

*"I believe that this nation should commit itself to achieving the goal, before this decade is out, of landing a man on the moon and returning him safely to earth."*

This ambitious aim was actually achieved with the Apollo mission 11 in 1969. The three astronauts Neil Armstrong, Edwin" Buzz" Aldrin, and Michael Collins set forth on July 16, 1969, in a Saturn-V-Rocket from the Kennedy Center in Florida and achieved on July 19 an orbit around the moon. The next day Armstrong and Aldrin landed on the moon in the moon capsule Eagle while Collins remained in the moon's orbit. A few hours later Armstrong became the first man to walk on the moon, followed by Aldrin. Neil Armstrong pronounced the sentence famous at the time, *"That's one small step for a man, but one giant leap for mankind."*

American president Jimmy Carter and the ailing Brezhnev signed a comprehensive disarmament agreement (Salt II) in 1979 in Vienna. However, the US Senate refused to sign it because of the invasion of Soviet troops in Afghanistan in December 1979. Thus began a new period of armament.

Less well known to most people in the West than the military might of the Soviet Union was the economic decline that began in the nineteen sixties and the end of all growth that began in the nineteen eighties. Technical innovation also began to stagnate. It was not known to me either that because of the information blockade in the West there was no reliable source of information concerning the Soviet economy. In addition, possible economic deficiencies were overshadowed by the dangers of the Cold War.

In his book, "The West and the Rest of the World," the brilliant historian Niall Ferguson writes that the CIA (1985), when Michael Gorbachev became the general secretary of the Communist Party of the Soviet Union, erroneously estimated the size of the Soviet economy to be about 60% of that of America. He states that the Soviet nuclear arsenal was actually larger than that of the United States. Harvard professor Ferguson states further, "If the Cold War had ever become hot, the Soviet Union would very probably have won." For one thing, its political system was far more able to compensate for heavy war losses; in the Second World War there were fifty times as many Soviet deaths in relation to those before the war in comparison to American deaths. For another, the Soviet economic system was ideal for the mass production of highly developed weapons. In 1974 the Soviets possessed a much greater arsenal of strategic bombs and ballistic rockets. Scientifically they were only slightly behind. Moreover, they possessed an ideology far more attractive to post- colonial societies throughout the Third World, as it is now called.

The Soviet secret service, the KGB, with its gruesome methods, was strongly anchored in the consciousness of my generation. In the western newspapers the views of the official "Pravda" concerning political events were repeated. Other than that we knew very little about what was really happening in the Soviet Union. Not until Michael Gorbachev became the general secretary of the Communist Party, and later president of the Soviet Union, did we learn that he had tried in 1985 to overcome economic stagnation with the catch words Perestroika (economic reform) and Glasnost (openness). He began a development that under his successor Boris Yeltsin led to the end of Soviet communism. Unlike Gorbachev, Yeltsin did not want to rescue the Soviet economic system, but rather to destroy it.

Russian arms were the legal successor of the Soviet arms. At the beginning of 1992 Russia found itself with a catastrophic shortage of food coupled with the return of five hundred thousand soldiers to Russian soil. With a consistently negative attitude towards the military this led to a situation of organizational and psychological chaos. The minister of defense of the Russian Federation tried to call up every possible part of the population in order to assure that the Russian military potential in the long run would have the status of a military world power. This involved above all control of atomic weapons.

The Iron Curtain signified not only a political dividing line in the middle of Europe, but also a barrier against the free flow of news and information. Facts concerning events in Russia and in Eastern Europe countries under Soviet domination were sparse and had to be regarded with the greatest suspicion. In August 1968 as I experienced myself as a tourist, Leonid Brezhnev suppressed the Prague Spring forcefully with Warsaw Pact troops. Yet he allowed foreigners for the first time to drive in their own cars, but only on precisely specified roads: from Hungary over Kiev or from Poland by way of Smolensk to Moscow and Leningrad. These corridors, defined by the state tourist bureau Intourist, could only be traveled if a visa was stamped for a specific period. In addition, travelers were carefully observed by the KGB. In Switzerland it was known that such tourists were listed in an index of people who had made communist contacts in the east, which sometimes had a negative impact on a career.

Everybody in the west who experienced the Cold War in any form was impressed by the threat of the Soviet Union. It was clear to all of us that the communist leadership, while pretending to be government by the people, was in fact a dictatorship of a self-selected political elite. But we knew practically nothing about the life of a simple Soviet citizen, for the Iron Curtain did not allow a look into an authoritarian state with a collective economy. To be sure, there were individual left-leaning politicians, authors, and artists for whom going to the Soviet Union became a place of a sort of pilgrimage, giving them no dependable picture of the Soviet Union. These people hoped to see the first socialist state of workers and farmers, which to be sure gave them a distorted picture of socialism. Let us take just one example of these biased left-leaning intellectuals and artists who, as admirers of communism, made a pilgrimage to the Soviet Union: the great Chilean poet Pablo Neruda (1904–1972), who, said Hans Magnus Enzenberger (a German intellectual and an expert of Neruda's work), had "the most powerful voice in the Latin American continent." Yet according to the NZZ (August 8, 2011) Neruda had a second face which is usually suppressed today. The philanthropist extolled mass murder: "People of Stalin: we bear this name proudly!"

Stalin himself gave the key to his understanding through his credo: *"Choose one's victims, prepare one's plans minutely, slake an implacable vengeance, and then go to bed – there is nothing sweeter in the world."* According to careful estimates Stalin had forty million people on his conscience.

The few western businessmen who were traveling in the Soviet Union for foreign firms also had no overview, as they were constantly under surveillance and could only see what the government was prepared to show them.

Karl Eckstein, who settled in 1982 behind the Iron Curtain – when Brezhnev still ruled the Kremlin – wrote me something that did not quite agree with this opinion. "For instance, since 1982 I have often traveled around the Baltic States, when practically no one knew the names of Estonia, Latvia, and Lithuania. The problem is rather that we had no interest in first-hand information and reports from the Soviet Union were nothing but Kremlin astrology. The surveillance had in my time almost ceased to function."

Suddenly everything was different. In November 1989, to almost everyone's surprise, the Berlin wall fell, and, even more surprising, at the end of 1991, the Soviet Union ceased to be. The infamous Iron Curtain, only three hundred kilometers from Switzerland, was completely open. The unexpected possibility of getting an ideological view of the post-communist world, at that time at first only partly private, and of the communists, still well organized and with many adherents who hoped for a return to power, had for Dominik and me a tremendous attraction. Despite great hurdles we were motivated to experience personally the transition, regarded by the west as the "upheaval in time," and described as a decisive transition from the Soviet to post-Soviet Russia. The hurdles made this a risky enterprise, but at the same time it presented an irresistible temptation.

## Chapter 2

## THE ADVENTURE BEGINS IN MOSCOW

During my absence from the home office, at the beginning of 1993, while I was engaged in business trips abroad, a young man named Michael Alexandrov appeared at the Holderbank cement group, wanting to talk with management about investment opportunities for foreigners in Russia's cement industry. Together, with a group of his peers, this individual had bought some shares in Russia's cement industry for Alfa Bank's branch in Moscow, a possibility that had arisen in Russia during a period of privatization. Now he was looking for an industrial group *outside* of Russia for expanding the development of her cement industry on a more *global* level.

By default, as no one else at Holderbank had time for him, Alexandrov landed in the office of my very resourceful and forward-looking colleague, Dominik Wlodarczak – who, like me, was very interested in exploring the political and economic underpinnings that would support sound investments in Russia. Dominik filled me in on the interesting conversation he had had with this stranger, focused mostly on the possibility of cutting advantageous deals for our Swiss company concerning cement shares in Russia. In the course of conversation, Alexandrov had invited him to Moscow to discuss this topic further. As my colleague and I were fascinated by both the unique opportunity for doing business with the Russians and by learning more about the country generally (a country often referred to as the *workers' paradise*), we discussed going forward with fostering a reliable bond with this individual. Since we were in no way authorized to arrange cement acquisitions in Russia for our Swiss cement group, we contemplated making an exploratory trip to Moscow as counselors for a TACIS Project for the European Union; if not this, should we perhaps take a completely different political and economic approach. TACIS, a financial instrument of the EU, is an anagram for Technical Assistance to the Commonwealth of Independent States. It was founded in 1991 to support the connection of the EU with the countries of Eastern Europe and Central Asia through a program of technical assistance. The program supports the process of effectuating a transition to a market economy and the democratization of the countries in question. Switzerland could also participate in this development program.

Without giving exact information about our plans to promote and join a TACIS project in Russia, Dominik and I flew to Moscow in the spring of 1993. We had been rather nervous during this Swissair flight, for it had occurred just fifteen months following the dramatic fall of the Soviet Union; an event symbolically represented on December 31, 1991, when the red flag, with hammer and sickle, was removed from atop the Kremlin and replaced by the old Russian flag that had been used unofficially during the period of the Provisional Government, a period spanning the years from the fall of the czar to the October Revolution. Russia now stood at the threshold of an enormous economic, political, and social transformation – a time when there would be many losers and few winners. In this enormous land, populated by a broad spectrum of ethnicities, nobody knew exactly what direction this new political system would take.

The *officious* personnel we encountered while going through customs at the antiquated Sheremetyevo Airport, a transportation facility located near Moscow, seemed frightening to us. The excessive military protocols of the customs officers, especially with regard to examining our passports, conveyed an obvious distrust of foreign visitors, an expression of disapproval and suspicion much like the one conveyed by the East German soldiers I had encountered on my trip to East Berlin in the spring of 1965; on that occasion, at Checkpoint Charlie, I had been interrogated in a prolonged interview, with my passport scrutinized in every minute detail, as only a very dangerous political conspirator would expect. It seemed to us as though not much had changed with immigration and customs since Soviet times.

Fortunately, Michael Alexandrov had organized VIP service so that we were able to bypass the long lines for entry and be taken instead to a quiet spot where the custom procedures were somewhat abbreviated and less formal, allowing us to retrieve our luggage with relative efficiency. All it took to get VIP service, including the chance to converse with some influential people in a private room, was to purchase this special treatment with enough rubles or dollars, at that time amounting to about fifty dollars per person.

Alexandrov, along with his employees (who also worked in the Moscow branch of the famous Alfa Investment Fund) was waiting for us. Both he and his staff had come with their own cars and with the bank's chauffeur; for, as they explained to us, using one of the many available taxis would be far too dangerous for non-Russians. On the way into the city, evidence of the recent construction explosion was yet to be seen; but, on the edge of the city, we saw many tacky prefabricated apartment buildings; finally, upon reaching the center of the city, close to the hotel where our rooms were reserved, we confronted a chaotic pattern of traffic that challenged both drivers and pedestrians alike.

We settled into our rooms at the famous Metropol Hotel, a place that had been tastefully renovated by a Finnish firm. Here, once again, we felt safe and comfortable – in contrast to the initial sense of discomfort generated by the customs officers at the airport. The feeling experienced at the airport, I realized, stemmed largely from years of indoctrination, a general orientation engendered during my military service in the Swiss infantry, whereby the Russian soldier appeared as a dedicated warrior in the service of communism and the *Cold War,* an enemy of the free world, always coming *from the east.* Certainly, coming to the Metropol helped to offset these feelings.

The Metropol, one of the most beautiful hotels in Moscow, is rendered in the style of Art Nouveau. It became the setting for "Dr. Zhivago," a film made in 1965, starring Omar Sharif as the doctor and poet and Julie Christie and Geraldine Chaplin as his romantic interests. The choice location of the hotel, near the Bolshoi Theater in one direction and near the famous Red Square in the opposite direction, is an added attraction. In Red Square lies the body of Lenin, founder of the Soviet Union, where, since 1924, his embalmed body is displayed in a mausoleum at the wall of the Kremlin. Today, the hard-nosed critics of the communist system chuckle over the irony that Lenin, situated in a mausoleum that overlooks GUM Department Store, is forced everyday to lie in close proximity to the ultimate symbol of the decadence and elitism of a social class deemed as *the enemy of the people*, a social class against whom Lenin struggled all his life.

A brief excursion into Lenin's history is warranted here. After the February 1917 Revolution and the ousting of the czar, Lenin and other prominent communists returned to Russia from Switzerland with the support of the German top military brass, passing over the territory of the opponents – Germany, Sweden, and Finland. They traveled in a sealed train which was declared a possession of an extra-territorial area. From the first, Lenin stood against the provisional Russian government headed by the minister-president Alexander Kerensky, a member of the social revolutionary party. Kerensky's government officially banned the Bolshevik Party and its major press organ, Pravda. Because of this pronouncement, Lenin feared the death sentence and went underground. In November 1917 (October in the Julian Calendar, a calendar still used in Russia) the Bolsheviks and the newly-established Soviets succeeded in bringing down the liberal-socialist coalition government with their storming of the Winter Palace in St. Petersburg, at that time the capital during and following the October Revolution. Kerensky fled to exile, in France. Leo Trotsky, Lenin's confidante, organized the uprising on the twenty-fifth of October. It met with little resistance, as Kerensky's government, with inadequate military support, retreated to the Winter Palace. A council of commissaries (Soviets) transferred power to Lenin, making him the premier.

Lenin's death in 1924 led to a bitter struggle over succession, a struggle eventually won by Joseph Stalin over Leo Trotsky. Trotsky had been the major organizer of the Russian Revolution and had led the Red Army to victory in the civil war. Throughout his life, Trotsky had fought bitterly against Stalin; but by 1929, he was driven out of the Soviet Union, reaching Mexico by way of Turkey, France, and Norway. The precautions needed to effectuate his safety presented him with great financial problems. Finally, a Soviet agent who had become engaged to Trotsky's secretary managed to get into his house and to pierce his skull with an ice pick – an instrument of death since made famous. Thus, in 1940, in Mexico, Stalin had his challenger murdered in cold blood.

The supreme leaders of the Soviet Union, stodgy and impervious men serving as members of the politburo, stood on the platform of the mausoleum, playing their expected role in the annual May First Military Parade. The ranking of the members of the politburo, at that time, was in accordance with the division of power in the Kremlin. It gave me chills each time I saw on television during the Cold War Years these evil old men in their overcoats and hats, doling out an approving look to the troops parading past them and giving an additional nod of respect to the heavy weapons they carried – particularly to the enormous intercontinental rockets.

Even back in the time of the czars, the troops paraded through Red Square. In the fourteenth century the grand dukes lived in the Kremlin; today the president of Russia lives there. Within the walls of the Kremlin, along with fortifications, are a number of sacred and secular structures stemming from various times. Russia's seat of government sits on a twenty-eight hectares (70 acres) triangle, forty meters (44 yards) high, in the middle of the city. Red Square made a great impression on me every time I visited Moscow. The architectonic interplay of St. Basil's Cathedral, the History Museum, the GUM Department Store (which in Soviet times was used as the measure of production of material goods), and the Kremlin Wall – the entire architectural mix contained in Red Square – is one of the most impressive sights that Moscow has to offer, giving a sense of the whole of Russian history. Here I began to rethink matters; I began to overcome my antipathy against all things Russian, a negative impression implanted in me during the Cold War, a period during which many brutal incidents were enacted, largely under the domination of the Soviet Union. Despite these negative memories, something new was taking hold of me, something that was triggering in me a fascination with the *Russian soul*.

Sometime later, in the office of the well-known Moscow Branch of Alfa Bank, we met Simeon Kharif, Director of the Gornosavodsk Cement Factory (an establishment situated in the Urals – three hundred kilometers (186 miles) from Perm). As we soon became aware, this man had an impressive network of contacts in the Russian cement industry as well as in the government. He was connected with Yegor Gaidor, the Minister of Economics who, subsequently, became the Commissary-Minister-President. In order to effect significant business transactions in Russia, one had to have a network of important business contacts, such contacts as could be found among the members of the so-called *Siloviky*, as well as among members of the military and secret services. As we gradually discovered, Kharif had been the representative of the Perm District in the Soviet Parliament but, as a Jew, his prospects for a major career seemed limited, with the assignments offered him proving difficult – such as reflected in his appointment to the position of Director of Operations in Yakutsk, a place located in deepest Siberia. With the fall of the Soviet regime and the rise of a new wave of liberalization and privatization, he suddenly found a milieu in which he could prove his abilities and undertake enterprises of his own choosing. To maximize the possibilities of this new freedom, he turned his attention to a whole host of cement factories in which he might like to participate. Kharif formed a fifty percent partnership with Alfa Bank using Alfa-Bank money – an appropriate move in light of the rush to privatize a number of cement factories and acquire shares in them. On his team he had a number of long-term associates from the cement industry, people who continued to support him in his new ventures.

When we first made contact with Kharif, his attention was concentrated on forming an alliance with the Investment Fund of Alfa Bank, a fund which held vouchers for the purchase of shares in the Gornosavodsk Cement Factory. This capital had already been used for purchasing a small number of vouchers for the Volsk Cement Factory (located in the Saratov region on the Volga), as well as for purchasing vouchers for the Nishni Tagil Mill and the Shigulevsk Cement Factory, the latter two located in the Urals. From the first, we were impressed with the extensive holdings of the Investment Fund, but we demanded, nevertheless, some changes be made, to wit: acquiring an increased number of shares in Volsk Cement, as well as acquiring new shares in Shurovo Cement (near Moscow) and the Spassk Exporting Firm (near Vladivostok). On the downscaling side of the coin, we proposed the sale of shares in non-strategic minor factories, namely Nishni Tagil and Shigulevsk, both in the Urals. It was the intention of our two Russian contacts, Kharif and the Alfa Bank Investment Fund, to establish a strong holding company through which it could purchase more shares in other cement works. For us, their combined access to people in high places was an attractive asset worth serious consideration, viable partners for our client, Holderbank, the mechanism through which more shares could be acquired. It provided Holderbank some assurance that any investments they made in the Russian cement industry would be handled safely and efficiently by people well-versed in the oddities of the Russian way of doing business, an unspoken code fraught with danger for the uninitiated. And Holderbank, from the standpoint of the two Russians, would be the mechanism through which more shares could be acquired. Yet for all parties concerned, this partnership between east and west was new territory, politically, economically, and legally. Over-riding the uncertainties posed by a new kind of partnership was the determination of Alfa Bank and Kharif to seize the opportunity for untold profits, an opportunity arising in what might be a very short-lived period of privatization, when other interest groups were scrambling for the rewards, achievable only by those who acted quickly.

Somehow our hosts felt a gold rush atmosphere such as must have prevailed in 1848, at the beginning of the Gold Rush in California. To be sure, in comparing the gold rush in present-day Russia with its California predecessor, one finds important differences: in the California Gold Rush of 1848, the principal fortune-hunters were poor and unemployed immigrants, people who desperately dug for gold nuggets with crude instruments – i.e., with shovels, spades, sieves, and even with their bare hands. In Russia, on the other hand, the fortune hunters consisted of the well-educated and well-connected, overall, a somewhat elite population, determined to seize a one-time opportunity for wealth spawned by capitalism and the new system of privatization.

To be sure, the gold rush atmosphere was prevalent only in the center of Moscow, where a new spirit of exuberance took hold. Replacing the austere communist fog that had settled over the city for so long was a new environment, colorful and even *glitzy* in so many respects: an explosion of new construction, bustling restaurants and bars, a flood of western consumer goods, shrill advertisements and neon signs, ostentatious luxury limousines, an increase in traffic – all these things seemed to announce a vibrant and glorious future – a dynamic made palpable mostly in the heart of Moscow. It was here that the boundless energy of an awakening giant was most keenly felt.

Everything was possible in this chaotic period of transition, from communism to a still-unclear new order. The economic cards were newly dealt. Anyone who was clever, unscrupulous, and fast enough could quickly acquire a fortune. Mikhail Fridman, who at thirty-five had founded the Alfa Bank (the Alfa Investment Fund was a subsidiary) stands as a prime example of the newly arising elite that was competing for power and social status with the old apparatschiks.

Together with Pjotr Aven, Fridman was the principal founder of the Alfa Group. He was also the most active player and the Chairman of the Board of Directors of the Alfa Group, one of the most powerful private industrial and financial concerns in Russia. Today he is considered one of the most influential industrial leaders in Russia and one of the most significant Russian oligarchs. His partner, Pjotr Aven, whom, later, we also got to know, was a colleague of Yegor Gaidar during their student days, a man who later became Prime Minister. Gaidar is considered the architect of the controversial 1992 shock therapy reforms). At the beginning of the nineteen-nineties, Aven was the Russian Minister for Foreign Trade; later he was the director and influential top man at the Alfa Bank, where he remains today.

The weakening of the old civil order and traditional institutions brought freedoms hitherto unknown, but it also created unintelligible and confusing situations which fortune seekers of various types tried to exploit in their chase after quick money. This atmosphere presented numerous challenges to the honest business men from Switzerland who had no experience and no network in Russia. Back then, and still today, choosing the right local partners was the key to successful business dealings. These partners had to have good political and economic connections in Russia; they needed to have a precise knowledge of the interconnections of political influence and how to make creative and unorthodox use of them to their own advantage. Not least, they needed to be loyal to their clients or partners in the West. Only with these stipulations in place was there a chance to assert themselves amidst the Russian chaos and make a successful business arrangement among the possibilities offered. It turned out later that we had had the good fortune to have found just such partners in Simeon Kharif and the Alfa Bank. Without them, we would not have succeeded in compiling viable shares in the Russian cement industry, free of the usual, unforeseen hazards.

Once we expressed the desire to see an actual voucher, the representative of the Investment Fund took us to a small windowless room at the back of his office, situated in one of the buildings on the Alfa Bank Campus. This room was filled practically to the ceiling with stacks of packets wrapped in paper, each packet containing 500 vouchers. As we had no idea how these vouchers found their way to the Alfa Investment Fund and what would happen to them next (with respect to privatization), Michael Alexandrov showed us a map of Moscow and its immediate environs. This map displayed all the collection points of the Alfa Investment Fund at which representatives of the Fund purchased vouchers intended for the workers and cadres, but only from *potentially interesting firms*. In other words, these distribution points absorbed the vouchers intended for *parties designated by the Investment Fund*. It was only after a while that Dominik and I came to understand the details of the part we played in the negotiations that took place during this early stage of privatization, a period that dated between 1992 and 1994. The chapter after the next will discuss this subject at greater length.

Next we were introduced to Pjotr Aven, the second-most important leader of the Alfa Bank. We were able to exchange a few words with the slender and elegantly dressed banker. With his polished appearance and good English he could have easily passed for a banker at a major Wall Street bank in New York. At his disposal, we noticed, was a black car fitted with a blue light atop its roof, a vehicle provided by the bank. As a former minister and immensely wealthy man, Aven was still allowed to use this status symbol. Only after one has driven on the Moscow streets can one appreciate the great benefit of access to such a vehicle. Without the beloved and much-envied blue light, short distances of five to ten kilometers can take two to three hours to traverse; with the light, by contrast, traffic, no matter how clogged, is miraculously cleared. As in Soviet times, policemen are posted at every main crossing in the middle of Moscow as well as at major exits of the roadway where there are special lanes for VIPS riding in vehicles equipped with blue lights; for these select few, policemen immediately stop the traffic to clear them on their way.

In Soviet days, members of the central committees of the communist party and the orthodox patriarchs drove custom-made SILs, (in English – ZILs, an abbreviation for Sawod Imeni Lenina Factory, a name for Lenin-Cadillac copies). Ministers and members of the party cadre drove large Tschaikas (Seagulls), the second-most luxurious limousine. On the street, these were known as *Hooligans*. The members of the class structure one rank down from ministers and members of the party cadre drove black Volgas, whose exterior bore a certain resemblance to a Mercedes. And finally, the great masses considered themselves fortunate if, after waiting for years, they could buy a Schiguli or the cheaper Saparchez, both, essentially, a copy of the Fiat. Abroad, the Schigulis were called Ladas. The production of Ladas was begun in 1970 at the plant AutoNAS in Togliatti, a new city named after the Italian leader of the Communist Party, Palmiro Togliatti. The oligarch Boris Beresovski became rich thanks to corrupt plant managers in the auto industry. He paid $3,500 (USD) for a car whose production costs were $4,700; then sold the car for $7,000.

At the beginning of the nineties there were still many makes of cars from Soviet days:
Ladas, Volgas, and Schigulis, but also used Opel Vectras and old Fords. Later these cars were hardly to be found. Typically seen on the street were armored Audi A8s, S-class Mercedes, BMW-7s, and a legion of dark companion SUVs. Every now and then even a fashionable Maybach was to be seen.

Voucher (share certificate)

## Chapter 3

## THE END OF THE SOVIET UNION 1991

The crisis in the Soviet Union grew greater and greater during 1991. The shortage of supplies led to disastrous consequences. There was too little food and, consequently, a great wave of strikes in the coal districts, hastening the downfall of the Soviet Union. Moreover, the national conflicts in the Caucasus turned into open war. At this point it is worthwhile to take a more intense look at this fateful year. On August 8, 2011, German Radio wrote into the program, "How the Soviet Union Collapsed Twenty Years Ago: In August 1991 the communist hardliners attempted a putsch against the Soviet reformer Michail Gorbachev. They wanted to prevent the fall of the Soviet Union, but their efforts brought about the opposite."

It was either all or nothing. In 1991 the Soviet Union found itself in free fall. Industrial production declined, the unemployment rate rose, and galloping inflation devoured the citizens' savings. Ethnic conflict erupted; there was shooting in Georgia and Azerbaijan. In 1990, Lithuania became the first Soviet republic to declare independence. In January, Moscow sent a KGB super-commando (ALFA) to Vilnius. Fourteen people died when the television tower in the Lithuanian capital was stormed; but the attack did not succeed in bringing Lithuania back into the Soviet Union. President Michail Gorbachev increasingly lost control over his land.

In March 1991, Gorbachev held a referendum. According to the official report, more than seventy percent voted for retaining the Soviet Union as a renewed federation of sovereign republics with equal rights. Discussions in Gorbachev's residence, situated in the vicinity of Moscow, were inconclusive. Only nine of a total of fifteen Soviet republics participated. After several deliberations, the republics agreed to a new union treaty which was to make the independent republics into a federation with a common president, a common foreign policy, and a common military. The signing was scheduled for August 20, 1991, but did not take place. On August 19, one day before the planned signing, a group of Soviet hardliners formed an "emergency committee"; this included the defense minister, the minister of the interior, and the head of the secret service (KGB). All were members of a conservative junta of the reactionary wing of the communist party of the Soviet Union. A planned attack on the government building by ALFA, the military unit of the KGB, failed when the members of the unit unanimously refused to carry out the command. The conservative junta organized a coup, removed the president of the country. The putschist declared in a communiqué of the news agency TASS that Gorbachev got sick and therefore had to be removed from all his political duties. In reality Gorbachev was with his family at their vacation home in Foros/Krim. On August 18$^{th}$ 1991 Gorbachev was completely locked up in his house and the communications with the outside world were capped after he refused to approve the state of emergency and to render all his powers to the Vice President.

But August 1991 proved to be the golden hour of Boris Yeltsin who presented himself as the opponent of the communists. Ten thousand people gathered before the White House, his official residence in Moscow, to demonstrate against the putsch. Two military regiments of the putsch switched sides and came to defend the White House, their weapons pointed outwards. When Yeltsin heard about this, he left the government building and climbed aboard a tank. Standing on the tank, he effectively condemned the attempted overthrow. After three days, the putsch finally collapsed, its members arrested; additionally, Yeltsin banned the communist party. Gorbachev returned to Moscow as president of the Soviet Union, resigning his position as general secretary of the communist party of the Soviet Union.

After the putsch was quelled, the Soviet Union finally collapsed. One after the other, the non-Russian republics declared their independence from the Union of Soviet Socialist Republics. Politically strengthened, Yeltzin took control of the media and the key ministries. On December 8, in Minsk, the presidents of Russia, the Ukraine, and Belarus signed a document declaring the dissolution of the SovietUnion, replacing it with the Community of Independent States (GUS). Yeltsin informed the US president, George Bush, by phone and put the White Russian president, Shushkevich, in touch with Michail Gorbachev, the President of the Soviet Union. Gorbachev reacted harshly, speaking of a coup d'etat and calling Yeltsin a traitor, but he was no longer able to rescue the Soviet Union. On December 21, the representatives of the Soviet Republics confirmed the end of the Soviet Union in the Protocol of Alma-Ata (Kazakhstan). With the exception of three Baltic states and Georgia, all the republics agreed to the "Commonwealth of Independent States" (NZZ August 12, 2011). Step-by-step, Yeltsin demoted Gorbachev, depriving him of his former powers. On December 25, 1991, Gorbachev withdrew from his position as the highest official of the one-time super-power. On December 26, the Soviet Parliament confirmed the effective dissolution of the Soviet Union. Under Yeltsin's leadership, the USSR forfeited its rights to the Russian Federation. The Soviet Union had collapsed, an empire which previously had inspired great fear throughout half the world. On December 31, 1991, the red flag with hammer and sickle which had flown over the Kremlin since 1918 was finally lowered forever.

## Chapter 4

PRIVATIZATION – A SYSTEM BUILT ON VOUCHERS AND AUCTIONS
1992 TO 1994

The *Period of Privatization* was an era whose economy was built on a system of vouchers and auctions. The young reformers in the government were of the opinion that every private owner of a Russian establishment would be more efficient than the state in protecting his investment by demanding the necessary legal safeguards to do so. Private owners in the same industry would compete for profits, thereby raising the value and quality of their individual companies which, in turn, would stimulate the entire economy. In this phase of privatization, the most valuable public companies – gas, oil, and minerals – would be excluded from the process of mass privatization.

Every Russian citizen was offered a voucher, i.e., a certificate of ownership. It could be exchanged for shares in a private firm, invested in a voucher fund, or sold for cash. Direct exchange for shares was to take place at a voucher auction in which the owner of the vouchers could offer them for shares. In December 1992, beginning with the Bolshevik Biscuit Company, the Russian government began to auction off shares in state companies. The reformers attained their goal of rapidly privatizing a large number of state enterprises. Between January 1992 and June 1994, the government released 16,500 firms to free competition, making forty-one million Russians shareholders, either directly or through a voucher investment fund. Given the great rapidity with which the privatization process was enacted, many citizens did not understand exactly what was involved and could not adequately profit from the process. Moreover, the auctions took place throughout the country and some were not sufficiently advertised. Anatoly Chubais, who was responsible for carrying out privatization through several phases, made the following comment about the emerging business elite:

"They steal and steal and steal. They are stealing absolutely everything and it is impossible to stop them. But *let* them steal and take their property. They then will become owners and decent administrators of this property."

Elsewhere in this book will be described the completely different type of privatization that took place from 1995 to 1997, a sort of silent privatization called, "pledge auctions".

Andreas Born presented, in an easily comprehended book, the phase of privatization that took place between 1992 and 1994, his study appearing under the title, "Russia and Oligarchs: Privatization, Vouchers, Certificates of Ownership."

"Privatizing of the state–owned Russian firms was at the top of the reform agenda when, in October 1991, Anatoly Chubais assumed responsibility for the State Committee on the Management of State Property (GKI). Top priorities in Russia were liberalizing prices and controlling the budget. Yet politicians and the public were discussing whether there should be privatization *at all* and whether macro-economic problems should not be solved first.

At the beginning of 1992 the leading reformers, Yegor Gaidor and Anatoly Chubais, initiated so-called *shock therapy* for fixing the economy. By liberalizing prices, while at the same time introducing private ownership, they endeavored to rid Russia of state-supported enterprises. Against the opposition of the old Soviet managers, they wanted to privatize the worn-out state enterprises and set into motion a dynamic revolution. This, they thought, would strike a final blow to communism.

There being a shortage of western-trained managers, the reformers were forced to work with the old managers. A tested means was the voucher system of privatizing. The state-owned enterprises were changed into private companies and the shares were distributed, partly to the co-workers, but principally to the old managers. This ended the opposition to privatizing.

Originally Chubais wanted to give forty percent of the shares of a firm to the workers and directors, but the directors' lobby, particularly the lobby led by Arkady Volksky, set the quota at fifty-one percent. Studies showed that, in fact, an average of sixty to sixty-five percent of the shares went to the management. Twenty percent went to individuals and to voucher funds. The rest remained in state hands.

On January 10, 1992, the distribution of one hundred forty-eight million vouchers, with a face value of ten thousand rubles (about thirty Euros) began. Every citizen had the opportunity to acquire vouchers; but, due to the poor economy, the good idea of spreading state wealth as broadly as possible among the population was destroyed. Most citizens could not get together the increasing prices (hyperinflation) needed to pay for everyday necessities. So it is hardly surprising that many citizens traded in their vouchers for cash, with the result that the price for the vouchers fell drastically.

Most of the vouchers were sold on the black market or were drawn into so-called *voucher funds*, many of which were founded for dishonest purposes. The purchasers then simply retained the fund certificates. Many voucher funds were found to be disguised funds through which firms bought their own shares. Ninety-nine voucher funds, and the funds on which they were based, simply disappeared from the scene.

The big winners were the Red Directors (the old managers) or the members of the old Soviet elite. These managers of the state-combines often transferred firm monies in large quantities to their subsidiary firms and then used that money to buy up the certificates of their combines.

Other powerful groups were the black market entrepreneurs and criminals who used their assets to purchase vouchers, thus laying the foundation for a legal financial empire. The early pioneers, founders of cooperatives, as well as the wandering dealers and brokers, had access to large sums of money of which they made advantageous use in taking control of the firms that were previously state-owned.

The vouchers were offered by the government to ordinary people for free. Altogether, all the vouchers were worth only about twelve billion USD and, with that, most of the state enterprises in Russia were privatized. At auctions, the vouchers could be exchanged for shares. As foreigners could not participate, the shares sometimes had a ridiculously low value.

The general monopoly known as Gazprom, with enormous reserves of natural gas, was partially privatized, and control of this privatized portion went into the hands of the old managers for twenty-two point eight million US dollars; the enormous car company ZIL, with one hundred thousand workers, was privatized for sixteen million US dollars; the Volga car company for twenty-seven million US dollars; but the leading machine company, Uralmash, cost the later oligarchs Bendukids only four million US dollars.

The vouchers, however, also played a political role. In hindsight, even the then vice-president and father of the voucher system, Anatoly Chubais, had to admit that privatizing vouchers brought about little of the hoped-for significant redistribution of state enterprises among the general population. The true aim, nonetheless, was not economic, but rather political. The privatizing was supposed to appeal to the workers by giving them a stake in their own labor. The certificates of ownership were to foster a peaceful transition from communism to capitalism and were thought of as "… a weapon against the communist party."

By September 1993, more than twenty percent of Russian industrial workers were employed by private firms. Over sixty percent of the Russian population, it was estimated, supported privatization, an economic plan that came to be called *shock therapy*; and Chubais, as one of its founders and leading proponents, gained great visibility from the plan he devised, becoming one of Russia's best-known politicians of this era.

The Russian Congress of Deputies of the People granted Yeltsin the power to reform the administration of the Russian republic between November 1991 and December 1993. On August 19, 1991, President Boris Yeltsin, by decree, enacted the program of privatization. According to this decree, he, without parliamentary approval, could institute economic reforms and appoint ministers. Yeltsin seized this opportunity and declared publicly that the transition, while laborious for the citizens, would not take long. He assigned the task not to politicians, but to those he dubbed "professionals." Prominent among the "young reformers" was Anatoly Chubais, who had proved a tough negotiator as minister of privatization, and Yegor Gaidar, the intellectual leader of the group. Alfred Kokh also played an important role in the privatization process. All were professional economists under the age of forty. Some Russians complained that these young reformers, called upon to undertake the enormous task of introducing a market economy in Russia, were politically inexperienced. Echoing this idea, Alexander Rutskoi, the Soviet Vice-President of the Republic, described these young reformers as, "small boys in pink shorts and yellow boots."

From the first, the reformers planned to get rid of price controls, three quarters of the prices still being controlled by the state. They also had in mind liberalizing imports, a new tax structure, stabilizing the macro-economy, eliminating the budget deficit, and privatizing the majority of state-controlled firms. The rapidity with which these undertakings were to be accomplished led the populace to refer to the plan as *shock therapy,* a characteristic similar to what had happened in Poland. Originally Chubais favored rapid privatization, giving money to the state for the privatized firms. But the Congress of the Deputies of the People found this model unacceptable. Instead, on June 11, 1991, the Supreme Russian Soviet accepted as a compromise voucher privatization.

The reform team implemented its liberalization and stabilization plans with the help of the International Monetary Fund (IMF). By January 2, 1992, the government had already lifted price controls for most goods; and during the first months of 1992, the reformers attained some success. But in April 1992, half of the parliament, representing powerful political and economic forces, were opposing the tight monetary and fiscal policies which the government had imposed in order to fight inflation. The ensuing monetary devaluation and the effect on the population of the consequent rise of prices to a market rate caused a tricky political problem. As a result, the measures passed by the reformers were lost. The Central Russian Bank made the reform efforts more difficult by introducing a liberal credit policy for the various businesses. In June 1992, President Yeltsin nominated Victor Geraschenko to the position of Chairman of the Central Bank. Geraschenko, too, offered generous credit to the Russian businesses that were finding themselves in trouble. Thus it was no longer possible to tackle inflation. Not until July 1995 did inflation fall to under five percent, a level that it held until the financial crisis of August 1998.

After the two phases of privatization, Yeltsin, in 1996, appointed Anatoly Chubais to the title of Chief of Staff, a key position in the Moscow power structure. Then, in 1997, the state chief made him the Vice Premier (1997–98) under Viktor Chernomyrdin. When he left the political world, Chubais became the president of the state energy-combine known as United Energy System (1998–2008), one of the most powerful combines in Russia. This firm produced seventy percent of the electricity in Russia, employing four hundred and seventy thousand employees. In a 2007 interview with the magazine Der Spiegel, Chubais explained that many legal and technical mistakes were made during privatizing. But, he added, the most important point should not be forgotten – that privatization *did* come about. And it should also not be forgotten that in Soviet days private ownership was a crime, punishable by five years' imprisonment. Today, sixty percent of the economy is in private hands; and this has created the basis of growth. What was done was not ideal, but it averted a greater catastrophe and there was no civil war.

In an interview with Novagazeta (April 4, 2011), the then leader of the Central Bank, Victor Geraschenko, gave, among other comments, the following explanation: "Russia's *independence* began as mass robbing of savings from the population. In that situation I managed to insist on an urgent meeting with Gorbachev's office and explained the absurdity of Yeltsin's idea. Gorbachev had to agree and I ordered him to re-write the law! So, for one year, we averted economic collapse and the great robbery of the people; and some people got hurt. After the putsch against Gorbachev of 19 August 1991, I was fired, though one year later I was invited back.

In August 1992, the Head of the Central Bank failed to prepare a competent annual report of the bank's performance during 1991. So Boris Yeltsin just fired him. And I and my assistant had to restrain the uncontrolled inflation of 2100% created by the tricks of people who called themselves 'reformers.' The 'reformers' did not want to understand that it was not possible to cancel the deposits put into savings accounts but, instead, to index them after the first quarter of 1992 and not humiliate and rob their own people.

Next time I got fired was when they realized that the traditional tricks of Berezovsky didn't work with me and my assistants. Berezovsky, when he enters someone's office, likes to write big figures, like one million dollars, on a sheet of paper. And when the official develops *grasp reflex*, it's easy to tell him what to do."

## Chapter 5

OUR SECOND TIME IN MOSCOW
SEPTEMBER 1993

At the end of September 1993, Dominik and I flew to Moscow again and conducted business with the authorized staff of the Alfa Bank. We had prepared ourselves thoroughly for these talks and, in the meantime, had arranged to meet with the Holderbank executive committee member responsible for Europe, Andreas (Tres) Pestalozzi. Thanks to various talks with representatives of the investment funds during our first trip to Moscow, we knew the aims of the hoped-for collaboration with Holderbank. To prepare for the second round of negotiations, Dominik bought three large maps showing the provinces of the former Soviet Union and painstakingly glued stickers identifying the location of every cement factory in this huge country. For each factory, he included information about their capacity, workings, and so forth. This thorough preparation proved most helpful in our renewed negotiations. We met at various places, sometimes, as before, with Mr. Kharif. In the meantime, he had acquired two co-workers and a pretty secretary and had established government offices in Moscow, in the centrally-located Novy Arbat Street, an area characterized by the ugly architecture associated with the Khrushchev era. It was quite obvious that the Alfa Investment Funds had chosen Kharif to head the collection center for their cement enterprises. Thanks to Kharif, the Alfa Fund obtained vouchers, as rapidly as possible, not only from Gornosavodsk, but also from many other cement factories. Also, it quickly became clear to us that we needed to persuade the authorized combine leadership to embark on serious negotiations before our competitors did so. But this was no simple matter, as almost no one in Switzerland yet believed in positive developments in Russia. Ulrich Schmid, the correspondent from 1991 to 1995 for the influential Neue Zürcher Zeitung, spoke mostly just about the political power struggles at the highest levels of government and the ubiquitous Mafia. Thus few Swiss business concerns could work up enthusiasm for investing in Russia at that time. Andreas (Tres) Pestalozzi, the member of the Executive Committee for Europe, and thus also for Russia, was actually quite skeptical, yet he was willing to listen to our arguments. Above all, he was willing to come with us to Russia to form, in person, a picture of the complex, yet probable future possibility of obtaining many shares in a significant number of cement factories with just a little money.

With each visit, Kharif and the representatives of the Alfa Investment Fund became more confident, promoting their vision for western business investments in Russia with specific numbers. In order to paint a picture that compared the risks and opportunities involved in doing business in Russia, we began to make independent contacts and hold talks with people who already had experience with Russia, for instance, with leading co-workers of the firm ABB, Schindler, or Credit Suisse. Conversations with the Swiss Dr. Karl Eckstein, a veteran at negotiating business deals in Russia, were particularly interesting and helpful. He had studied law in Basel and had been active in Moscow since 1982. Since 1986, he had worked in a counseling firm that advised and supported western European firms active in negotiating contracts with the Russians that rested on matters pertaining to law and business. It became clear to us how well integrated he already was in Russia when he showed us the new offices he was planning to occupy. In the middle of Moscow, on the grounds of the freight (railway) station, Brezhnev had built a *secret* government station. It was completely finished, but was never used and appears on no maps. In all the upheaval, this station was completely overlooked; no authorities had paid any attention to it. Eckstein took this opportunity to acquire his new office, a place situated in a choice location, the middle of Moscow, and comprised of an entire complex of imposing halls and rooms.

With great pride, he showed us through the rooms and explained his plans for furnishing them; he had struck up a deal with the station officials for renting the furnishings. Of course none of this was official. Although the authorities paid no attention to it, it was a win-win situation for everyone involved to have the station put to good use, rather than letting it fall apart.

Eckstein impressed upon us how to do business in Russia. The weakened structures of official authority opened up undreamed-of possibilities to those who, with much creativity and vigorous determination, saw how to use this laxity in the enforcement of the old rules. Because the old institutions barely functioned or did not work at all, one had to take matters into one's own hands. A power vacuum of this sort, of course, offers the perfect breeding ground for parallel structures such as the Mafia to fill the void. Eckstein pointed out that, despite their power and terrorism, the Mafia was aware of functions that the authorities refused to take on. For example, when a stolen car needed to be retrieved, people went not to the police, but to the Mafia, who would actually look for it. The Mafia extorted money from ordinary citizens, but, in exchange, it gave them definite services. Such willingness of the Russians to compromise the basic standards of morality and ethics in the conduct of business would, predictably, pose a problem for the *high-minded Swiss businessman*. In order to feel at ease with the unorthodox methods encountered throughout the business culture of Russia, we needed trusted local partners to explain the intricacies and subtleties of this culture, a world only to be understood with some patience.

The Swiss elevator firm, Schindler, chose a different path. They appointed an Italian as business leader in Moscow, supposing that his Italian heritage would prepare him for coping with an intrusive Mafia presence and with the difficulties imposed by a weak civic order, certainly a leader whose background and experience would give him a decided edge over the *upright Swiss*. With our new contacts in Moscow, we gained a practical understanding of how to do business with the Russians. Additionally, we searched for local specialists who would be able to support us in structuring and transferring investments. We decided to work with the American law firm Chadbourne & Park, a firm that, a few years earlier, had established itself in Moscow with an elegant office. Our project was looked after by the head of the office, Robert Langer, an American who, having a Russian wife, had learned to speak fluent Russian. Many lengthy negotiations with the Alfa Bank and Kharif's team took place in the offices of Chadbourne & Park. At the beginning, their job was to construct an agreement concerning the basic structure of Holderbank investments; later, it was to work out settlements concerning shares. Robert proved to be a great asset. Along with his legal advice, his knowledge and experience with both western and Russian cultures helped us to better understand this country with its particular business behavior and legal system. It is also worth mentioning that the auditing firm, Arthur Andersen, made available IAS financial reports concerning all transactions.

Gradually we got to know our way around Moscow fairly well, beginning to feel at home and shaking off our prejudices about Russia. Alongside all the risks, uncertainties, and difficulties in the Russian economy, as portrayed very one-sidedly in the Neue Zürcher Zeitung, we began to see the many stories of success and the immense potential. We became convinced that there was a unique opportunity for a long-term investor such as Holderbank, a promising opportunity that far outweighed the risks. The ruling spirit of change again carried us to great plans for Holderbank, called Holcim since 2002; and we were determined to make use of the unique and probably never recurring opportunity to establish highly significant cement agreements for little money, albeit with some risk. Our assessment was supported by the excellent development of the earlier Russian cement market. Subsequently Holcim invested great sums in modernizing and developing the businesses they acquired at that time, particularly in Shurovo.

On a side street about ten minutes from the Metropol Hotel, I discovered an inconspicuous shop that had a relatively small window facing directly on the sidewalk; among other things, this seemingly modest shop offered Russian caviar – packaged in small bluish tins no larger than an ordinary bottle of shoe polish and costing no more than twelve US dollars. I remained faithful to this shop on my many return trips to Moscow. Once back in Switzerland, my wife and I enjoyed a special nighttime supper of bread, butter, caviar, and champagne. In buying caviar, one must be very careful not to be duped by tins filled mostly with an indefinable substance, topped with only a single layer of caviar. Many dishonest salesmen sell these tins to unsuspecting customers.

The second time I visited the shop, I decided to vary my evening walk by returning to the hotel via a different route. This path, following a course opposite in direction to the first one chosen, brought me to Lubyanka Place, once the central home of the KGB and the site of Lubyanka Prison, the most feared prison in the country. The Russian-Jewish writer and publicist Ilya Ehrenburg, a man who systematically incited the Russian army against everything German, rightly said of the prison and the KGB's tactics, one shivered, even in summer, when passing the Lubyanka Prison. During Stalin's reign of terror, but also later under Brezhnev, the Lubyanka was known as the first station on the way to being transported to Siberia. I automatically experienced the old reflex of fear thinking back on the days of the Cold War.

We sometimes ate breakfast in the hall of the elegant Metropol Hotel, a building done in the Art Nouveau style, topped with a large, colorful glass cupola dating from the Belle Epoch. Here in this hall, an attractive Russian woman with long blond hair played beautiful melodies on a harp, a performance that transported the listeners to a peaceful world. Reading the English-language newspaper, along with enjoying the outstanding service and the romantic atmosphere, we found ourselves in a buoyant mood. In the English-language newspaper published in Moscow we were constantly made aware of the power struggles in the government and the frightening presence of the Mafia. On one occasion, at breakfast, we learned of a Mafia businessman who, despite having five body guards, was shot to death. How was this possible? He was shot through the head by a hired assassin strategically positioned above him, as he and his five stocky, broad-shouldered, dark-suited, armed body guards descended the staircase into the metro. In such a situation involving an individual at high risk, it seemed better not to use body guards to protect the would-be prey of the assassin; for body guards are bound to draw too much attention to the person being *protected*. For many people in Moscow, there was great danger of death by an assassin's bullet. It was generally known that a killer could be hired for the mere sum of one hundred American dollars. The weak structures of the state led to the criminal take-over of many companies; indeed, corruption and contract killings were rife. In 1994 more than 600 entrepreneurs, politicians and journalists had been murdered.

The black market blossomed. The older generation was the major loser in the transition from communism to capitalism. As a result of the galloping inflation and the currency devaluation of the ruble, their savings and pensions lost almost all value. Understandably, many Russians longed for the old times that, relatively speaking, were more secure and stable under the communist regime than under the present economy.

To get to our various meetings in different parts of the city, we often had to take detours to avoid the military vehicles that usually surrounded the Russian Parliament (the White House) and the small group of troops that accompanied them. We asked our Russian companions what was really going on. It looked to us as though a new situation was developing, one incomprehensible and unfriendly to non-Russians. The representatives of the Alfa Investment Fund accompanying us reassured us that there was nothing to fear, and, in fact, life in Moscow seemed to be taking its normal course. We spent evenings in our favorite restaurant, Teatro, a gathering spot situated in the vaulted cellar of the Metropol Hotel, consuming good food with a bottle of red California wine (Woodbridge by Robert Mondavi). On the walls of the cellar were displays of the works of talented, young Russian artists; of a quality so good as it always prompted me to ask for a list of their names and the price of their works before looking at the menu. From the first, we noticed that almost all the food and bottled drinks served in the hotel came from other countries. The jam served at breakfast, for instance, was Hero, a Swiss product from Lenzburg. The restaurant was patronized not only by foreigners, but also by many Russian business men. They could be identified by their selection of whole bottles of vodka, instead of wine, that stood on the table. The "little water" was ordered in grams, not deciliters.

Since, as already mentioned, the Metropol Hotel was very near to the world-famous Bolshoi Theater, we used our few free evenings to visit this cultural Mecca. It struck me immediately that the time-honored 1825 theater needed renovation. The huge curtain, imprinted with hammer and sickle, was impressive and reminded one of the defunct Soviet Union of yore. The dancers of the Bolshoi, as well as of the Marinsky (in St.Peterburg) enjoyed world-wide recognition for their charisma and as technical virtuosos of their art, an acknowledgment that had made them icons of the Soviet Union's cultural achievements. Some of these world-renowned stars eventually defected to the west. Dominik and I had to pay greatly inflated prices for the tickets if purchased at the hotel; but if purchased on the black market, an operation camped directly in front of the theater, they were considerably cheaper. A performance at the world-renowned Bolshoi was always worth the cost, for the quality of the performances was consistently excellent. I was always delighted with the ballet, though a little less with the opera. At the time of my visit, the Bolshoi Opera was performing Boris Godunov, an opera with music by Modest Mussorgsky and a libretto based on Pushkin's drama of the same name. During intermission, on these visits to the Bolshoi, we always enjoyed a glass of Russian "champagne" – a libation to be had for the mere sum of five American dollars. American currency was gladly accepted everywhere. Among our observations of the ballets and operas we attended at the Bolshoi, we were struck by the fact that many more young people were in attendance at these events than would typically be found among audiences attending comparable performances in the west, the latter comprised largely of silver-haired patrons. An additional observation that attracted our attention was the fashionable attire worn by the young Russian women who attended these prestigious performances.

Six years later, in October of 2011, the magnificent Bolshoi Theater, an institution dating from the time of the czars, reopened its doors in renewed splendor. A major goal of the very costly renovation was to restore the damaged acoustics of the theater. Among other things, the orchestra pit was restored. In the nineteen twenties it had been filled with concrete.

When, after the performance, we had a nightcap at the bar of our hotel, we noticed a number of *ladies of the night,* their calling card consisting of their cheap attire and bright red lips. These young women, however, were neither intrusive nor aggressive. By contrast, as reported by a colleague staying at the Hotel Ukraine, his phone rang at midnight – when he heard the voice of a woman calling herself Natasha and speaking in a whisper – ask the western guest if he was feeling lonely.

## Chapter 6

## OMINOUS TENSION FILLS THE AIR

On September 28, 1993, when I was awakened by the hotel service, I turned on the television and saw on CNN the well-known British-Iranian journalist Christiane Amanpour, whose reports in 1990 about the Gulf War had brought her fame and had made her the most highly paid female reporter in the world. She wore a large floppy hat, was dressed for warmth (rather than glamor), and looked earnestly into the camera. I heard her explain on CNN that it was snowing in Moscow, which I found hard to believe given the mild weather the day before. To confirm her report, I pulled back the heavy curtains in my room and actually saw big snowflakes twirling around. Amanpour went on to say that the situation in the White House – then the home of the parliament, now the home of the government – had intensified dramatically. At first I thought that this was another exaggerated report from a sensation-hungry journalist and that CNN, too, had followed the trend of journalistic exaggeration in order to attract viewers to their televisions. At breakfast, I read the English-language Moscow newspaper and concluded that political tensions might have actually increased. After a brief conversation, Dominik and I decided to take the next available plane to Switzerland. The next day, September 29, we took a Swissair flight to Switzerland, although we were not sure we were making the right decision.

After the dangerous attempt at a putsch to overthrow the government, an event described in the next section of this book, our firm belief in the great investment possibilities for foreigners in Russia's cement industry and in her economic ascent out of stagnation was, for a time, rather shaken. What had actually happened after our flight? In a September 21, 1993 decree, President Yeltsin defied the constitution of the Supreme Soviet by dissolving the Congress of People's Deputies. The new parliamentary elections were set for December 12, 1993. On September 22, Yeltsin discussed with the prime minister, Viktor Chernomyrdin (1992–1998), the dismissal of the head of the Central Bank, Viktor Geraschenko, proposing in his place Boris Federov; but Chernomyrdin defended Geraschenko.

Along with the constitutional crisis precipitated by Yeltsin came another problem. The economic reforms were controversial and were strongly opposed by many members of parliament, as well as by bureaucrats and the directors of industrial enterprises – the so-called Red Directors. Some members of parliament refused to leave the parliament buildings, leading to a stalemate between the president and the parliament.

The parliamentary opposition then took over physical control of the White House. That is why, on several occasions, Dominik and I had seen troop-filled trucks stationed around the parliament building which forced us, upon leaving, to take a wide detour. The opposition named the vice-president, General Alexander Rutskoy, the new president. He was supported in this promotion by the Chechen, Ruslan Khasbulatov, the president of the parliament and one-time friend of Yeltsin. In the earlier 1991 putsch attempt against Yeltsin, he had taken the side of the successful opposition. In August 1991, Khasbulatov left the communist party and became, on October 29, 1991, the speaker of the Supreme Soviet. Yeltsin's September 21 unconstitutional dissolution of the Congress of People's Deputies caused a serious parliamentary crisis. Khasbulatov and the opposition remained in the White House and became Yeltsin's opponents.

At the beginning of October, the situation intensified dramatically. On October 3, 1993, armed followers of Khasbulatov and Rutskoy invaded the office of Moscow's mayor and attacked

The burning White House.

the Ostankino television station. Twenty-three people lost their lives. On October 3, Yegor Gaidor, the first vice-president under Viktor Chernomyrdin, on television, urged Yeltsin's followers to defend, unarmed, democracy and the Kremlin. Fortunately for Yeltsin, and perhaps for the free world, loyal troops marched in Moscow on October 4. The Russian White House was surrounded and came under fire from tanks. The White House began to burn and was attacked by Special Forces. More than one hundred people died. The rebels surrendered and the ringleaders of the putsch were arrested.

Just four days after returning to Switzerland, as I was watching Swiss television at home in my living room, I saw pictures of the upper stories of the parliament building burning while Special Forces, using helicopters, set down on the roof of the White House, lowered cables to repossess the great building – despite the fact that it was protected by more than three hundred heavily-armed rebel soldiers. It was impressive to watch the vice-president of Russia, Alexander Rutskoy, once a two-star general of the air force and a hero of the Soviet Union (who had also served as a pilot during the war in Afghanistan), leaving the building in battle gear, his hands up, under arrest along with Khasbulatov.

Both Rutskoy and Khasbulatov had deceived themselves. Both were convinced that the "silent majority" of the people and the army yearned for a return to past centralization and the old order, which in view of the rapid impoverishment of most of the population did not seem mistaken.

On October 5, 1993, the New York Times wrote about the attempted putsch of October 4 as follows: "Tanks and troops loyal to President Boris N. Yeltsin today crushed an armed uprising by his opponents with a potent show of force that left their riverside stronghold battered and in flames.

The Parliament building, known as the White House, was shaken by huge explosions from 125-millimeter shells fired from T-72 and T-80 tanks. As crack airborne troops conducted a floor-by-floor assault, hundreds of legislators, defenders and supporters began fleeing out of the building shortly before 5 P.M. Their leaders followed at 6 P.M.

Russian television showed Ruslan Khasbulatov, the Parliament chairman, and Aleksandr V. Rutskoy, a former general who had become the Vice President, grimly boarding a bus, Mr. Khasbulatov in his usual dark shirt and Mr. Rutskoy in camouflage fatigues.

About 30 prisoners, including Mr. Khasbulatov and Mr. Rutskoy, were taken to Lefortovo Prison in central Moscow where the Interfax News Agency reported they missed dinner. Mr. Khasbulatov and Mr. Rutskoy were given neighboring cells and were granted smoking privileges.

Mr. Yeltsin, apparently assured of the firm backing of security forces, moved quickly today to solidify his power. In addition to ordering the arrests, he banned some opposition parties, including the communists and nationalist organizations like Pamyat. He also closed many opposition newspapers, including Pravda, the former organ of the Communist Party.

For the moment, Mr. Yeltsin's actions seemed to command overwhelming support in Moscow and in the provinces, in large part drawing on widespread horror at the large-scale violence waged on Sunday by the opposition. In Sunday's fiercest battle, an attempt by the rebels to seize the television center, 62 people were killed, including a large number of civilians caught in the firefight …"

The above-named infamous Lefortovo Prison for political prisoners got its name from the Lefortovo Quarter, a place situated east of central Moscow, which was named for the Swiss admiral Francois le Fort, a close confidant of Czar Peter the Great whose unit was stationed in this part of the city. Francois le Fort, called Franz, had participated in a number of wars against the Ottoman Empire. As of 1695, he attained the rank of admiral of the Russian Black Sea Fleet. From 1697 to 1698, he accompanied the czar and advised him on a large European mission.

## Chapter 7

THE CRISIS IS PAST – REMINISCENCES

Four weeks later, on our next visit to Moscow, we asked Michael Alexandrov whether he and his colleagues had really had no fear of the danger of an overthrow when the White House was occupied. Alexandrov and his two companions readily admitted that they had worried greatly about Russia's future, but had not wanted to frighten us at the time of the crisis. When Dominik and I flew back to Switzerland, they had stored water and groceries in the trunk of their car to assure themselves of provisions in case it had been necessary to flee over the Finnish border to the west.

When in 1997 I participated in a conference on strengthening the economic connections between America and Russia, held in Boston at the John F. Kennedy School of Government, Harvard University, I was astonished to find one, Mr. Alexander Rutskoy, among the participants from the elite Russian delegation. He looked well and wore an elegant dark blue blazer. I was even more surprised at the fact that Mr. Rutskoy, the one-time vice-president of Russia, was participating as the Governor of Kursk Oblast (Province). In his presentation, he explained that he was personally promoting investments in his region and would definitely make sure that applications for foreign investments in Kursk Province would be addressed promptly. He would guarantee that such applications would be secure and would be of interest to foreign investors. I had a chance to have a brief personal conversation with this energetic, self-confident and seemingly cultivated man. I learned much later that he had been released from prison in 1994, when the new parliament granted him amnesty. Nonetheless, he continued to denounce Yeltsin and supported a reunification of Russia with the Ukraine and Belarus.

On the evening of the first day of the conference, with weather that was comfortable and fair, a dinner was held for all eighty participants and some guests at Antony's Pier Four, a seafood restaurant situated in Boston, directly on the ocean. Two buses took us to the harbor. This great restaurant, famous for its fresh oysters and, above all, for its excellent lobsters, sat on Pier Four, a loading platform no longer in use by ships.

The speech at dinner was delivered by the infamous Boris Berezovsky, at that time one of the richest new Russians (Novi Ruski). He spoke enthusiastically about the unique possibilities then offered to foreign investors in Russia. To give an accurate picture of the current scene, he stated, without hesitation, that it was only thanks to him that Boris Yeltsin won the presidency again in 1996. It became more than embarrassing when Berezovsky, for five minutes and in great detail, boasted how he had helped Yeltsin with significant amounts of money and, by use of the media – which he controlled, helped him win reelection. He said he continued to have great influence over the president and, via a direct line, always had access to him, a statement that unfortunately proved to be true.

How could such a man acquire such great riches so quickly? A mathematician by education, he was active in an institute responsible for *automation in the car industry,* and had connections with Avtovaz, the manufacturer of Lada. In October 1993, along with some managers from the Avtovaz Company, he founded the All-Russian Automobile Alliance, using the large number of shares he had acquired in its investment funds when Avtovaz had become privatized. Later, Berezovsky became the most important auto dealer in Russia. Ladas were known for their simple technology, comfort, and very low price. By 1994, Berezovsky was the principal comptroller of the television company ORT, the largest and most extensive channel of Russia. As the only channel, ORT could broadcast programs throughout the country, unimpeded by any competing networks. In that same year, he survived a bomb attack on his car, and, in the very next year, investigations against him were initiated concerning the murder of the director of ORT, Vladislav Listyev.

In the 1996 election campaign, Berezovsky actually *did* support the re-election of Boris Yeltsin to the presidency of Russia – with his ORT channel and financial contributions. Additionally, Berezovsky controlled shares in the oil firm Sibneft and in the airline Aeroflot. He initiated the so-called Band of Seven Bankers, a group of rich oligarchs who gave massive support to Yeltsin in his second contest for the presidency. After this election and during Yeltsin's second term, Berezovsky actually *did* have great influence on the president. Journalists sometimes named him the "father of the Kremlin", as he was one of the very few people who always had access to Yeltsin. The July 10, 2011 Financial Times stated, "In 1996 he boasted to the Financial Times that he and six other businessmen controlled half his country's economy. Today he lives in political exile in the UK, an avowed enemy of the Kremlin. He was a math professor who had created Russia's biggest car dealership. He survived in 1994 a car bomb that decapitated his driver …"

But after Putin, one-time head of the KGB, took over the presidency from Yeltsin at the end of 1999, forcing Yeltsin to retreat immediately, Boris Berezovsky began to have problems – as did all oligarchs who did not bow out from politics under President Putin. Also, Berezovsky had something Putin absolutely wanted: a national television channel. The president was uncomfortable with ORT's report of the sinking of the submarine Kursk, showing mourning widows, which undermined Putin's position. Clearly, the "grey eminence" had at last outlived his time. In August 2000, Berezovsky went into exile. He fled to England, where, ever since, he has taken shelter in a villa in affluent Surrey, a district south of London, guarded by former members of the French foreign legion. Russia has tried to extradite him since 2001, but Great Britain has not given him up. He sold some of his shares to Roman Abramovich, including shares in ORT, Aeroflot, and Sibneft. As reason for the pursuit of Berezovsky's arrest, his accusers point to his dishonest business transactions. Specifically, he is said to have embezzled the equivalent of 13 million US dollars from investors in his financial transactions with Lada during 2011. According to a notice that appeared in the Aargauer Newspaper of March 2011, the French authorities on the Cote d'Azur seized two yachts belonging to the Russian multi-millionaire, Boris Berezovsky. They indicated the worth of the yachts to be twenty million US dollars. The Russian legal authorities claimed deceit and money-laundering on the part of Putin's opponents – among whom Berezovsky was one.

According to Spiegel Online (October 4, 2011), the onetime friends and business partners, Berezovsky (sixty-five years old) and Abramovich (forty-one), are now sworn enemies waging a legal battle in a London court. Abramovich is a multi-billionaire, estimated by Forbes to be worth 13.4 billion US dollars, while Berezovsky's fortune is dwindling. The Financial Times (October 7, 2011) writes, "Mr. Abramovich was an orphan raised in an oil town in Russia's far north. In 1988 he had started a business making plastic ducks, subsequently turning to oil trading."

According to a new book, "Oh Man, Your Testosterone!," written by a professor of medicine, Dr. Oswald Oelz, one-time chief doctor in Zürich and a well-known mountain climber, Roman Abramovich, now the owner of the Chelsea Football Club, wanted to climb Kilimanjaro but had to be evacuated at four thousand meters because of mountain sickness. According to the magazine Mare, perhaps to psychologically compensate for his defeat on the mountain, he turned his attention to his yacht, the Eclipse, and lengthened it to 162.5 meters. It is now fifty centimeters longer than the Dubai, the ship belonging to the ruler of Dubai and, until then, the biggest yacht in the world. As we learn from Spiegel Online (May 10, 2011), Abramovich's yacht is so big, reminiscent of a crusader ship, that it could not dock at the Cote d'Azur and, instead, had to drop anchor in the sea at the Bay of Antibes. But this was no great problem; for the yacht of the second richest Russian has access to two helicopter- landing-places and carries on board three sports boats. The Eclipse, built in a Hamburg shipyard, is surrounded by secrecy. The technical press ascribes to the yacht protective equipment worthy of James Bond. It is said to control an anti-rocket system, as well as a subterranean entrance by means of which the ship's guests can come on board or leave discreetly on a three-seater mini-submarine. The yacht is supposed to have cost 850 million Euros and a full tank said to have cost about a million Euros.

Oelz's book adds that on October 3, 1993, on television, Yegor Gaidar urged the population and the army to support Yeltsin. Gaidar and Chubais are considered the two architects of the famous *shock therapy*. Today many Russians still hold Gaidar responsible for the very hard economic times suffered in the country in the nineteen nineties: massive unemployment and hyperinflation were the results. Other Russians praise him as the man who saved the country from total collapse. The director of the Columbia University Earth Institute, Jeffrey Sachs, who counseled the Russian government in the nineties, considers Gaidar the true intellectual leader of a number of political and economic reforms.

In June 1995 I participated in a very interesting "Russian Summer" in Moscow sponsored by the World Economic Forum (WEF). Chubais was present at a panel discussion and a meal following it. Other speakers included Sergueev, Khodorkovsky (then the richest man in Russia), Kivelidi, Yasin (Minister of Economics) and Yavlinski (Duma Representative).The Swiss ambassador Johan Bucher was also present and was praised in Gisela Tobler's book, "Russians are Different." She wrote, "The new ambassador, Johann Bucher (1995 to 1999), proved to be a great manager, who in nothing flat reorganized the embassy to be a perfect service provider and who had his staff in perfect order."

We, too, had a good experience with the new ambassador. After a meeting at the Swiss Embassy in Moscow, on a late autumn afternoon in 1995, with Tres and Cyrille Kisselevsky, whom I will introduce later, the busy ambassador Bucher explained he was inviting us to the Bolshoi Theater. As it would be practically impossible to get to the Bolshoi on time in the embassy's car, we would all go on the metro, which would take only about ten minutes. First we had to get tickets at the metro station near the embassy. The tiny ticket window, hardly more than a slit, was positioned at about the height of the ambassador's chest – so that he had to stoop slightly in order to speak with the somewhat aging ticket agent seated within. This was a typical example of the many remaining symbols of an unfriendly service culture still rooted in the Russian bureaucracy.

The metro made a great impression on me. All the stations, erected during the Stalin era, gave the workers an elaborate subway, reminiscent of the palaces built under the czars – structures studded with marble floors, crystal lamps, and towering pillars.

The Bolshoi performance of "Swan Lake" was terrific, a ballet that had debuted in 1877 and represents Tchaikovsky's most

The Russian Summit of the WEF (World Economic Forum), summer 1995 in Moscow. Chubais us third from right.

Dinner in the hotel Metropol in Moskow: K. Haefeli, A. Pestalozzi. C. Kisselevsky, Ambassador J. Bucher, Mrs. L. Kisselevsky.

noteworthy composition for ballet. "Black Swan," a popular film produced by Darren Aronsky, is a recent version of "Swan Lake." For her performance as Odette, Natalie Portman won an Oscar.

Conference at the University of Harvard (John F. Kennedy School of Government) 1997. At the lectern Alexander Rutskoi, Governor of Kursk Oblast.

## Chapter 8

ON-SITE EVALUATION OF VARIOUS CEMENT WORKS –
IMPLEMENTING THE CONCEPT OF "DUE DILIGENCE"
NOVEMBER–DECEMBER 1993

As I was not able to be there, Dominik Wlodarczak describes here the special trip he made to Russia with Marc Wurtz, technical director of the Holcim factories in France, and Hanno Göhlsdorf, a young engineer from the technical department of Holderbank Management and Consulting Inc., now known as Holcim Group Support.

"Once the political situation had quieted down and our Russian partner was able to indicate further progress in building the cement group, he indicated how the appropriate representatives of Holderbank might come to an agreement with the Russian delegation for an investment in Russia. At this point, we decided to conduct a limited *'due diligence'* investigation."

Due to the absence of liquidity and readily available funds, the Russian economy, at that time, functioned largely by means of barter, making it difficult to get a definitive picture of the financial situation of individual cement works. Nonetheless, we engaged the auditing company Arthur Anderson, to examine the books of the most important cement companies and draw conclusions according to IAS (International Accounting Standards). At the same time, we made a tour of all the selected plants in order to get a picture of the technical condition of these factories. The team for this trip included from Holderbank Marc Wurtz, the technical leader of Ciment d'Origny, and Hanno Göhlsdorf, from the technical department of Holderbank Management and Consulting. The latter, being an East German, he spoke Russian and, aside from assisting us with his technical knowledge, helped us with understanding Russian.

After a long trip to Perm, in the Urals, we met Kharif and a couple of representatives from Alfa Cement, as the cement group in Russia was now called. They accompanied us on our tour. We were welcomed into an empty, rented apartment in the headquarters of Alfa Cement. It was immediately apparent that much was improvised and that the firm did not yet have a real structure.

Undeterred, we headed for Gornosavodsk (190 km. north-east of Perm). There were three of us and, in two large Volga cars, our contingent rode through the snow-covered Urals, from Perm to the area of Gornosavodsk. By nighttime, we reached a small hotel in the middle of the woods, a place more comfortable than we would have anticipated in this remote region. It belonged to an energy concern that obviously had the means to invest in such infrastructure. On the next day we saw our first Russian cement work, in Gornosavodsk. The heavy snow disguised the true state of the plant.

Nonetheless, it did not escape our observation that things were falling apart throughout the plant and that the machines were kept in operation by the simplest, somewhat primitive, means. But the ovens, after all, were kept running and, the bottom line, the factory *was* functioning enough to produce and sell its cement. Over the course of two days, we inspected several things – the technical state of the machines, the situation with the raw materials, production and turnover statistics, organizational structure, and so forth. From a European standpoint, the Russian works were enormous. When the USSR dissolved and the economy had collapsed, Gornosavodsk, like all other cement works in the country, produced only a fraction of its potential, given its oversized dimensions. Aside from that, the lack of liquid assets was the main problem faced by Russian industrial enterprises. The majority of customers had very little cash to pay for the cement and offered all kinds of physical goods in exchange. As the goods offered in payment were not always useful, another recipient had to be found who could offer goods that were more applicable. Thus there came about a barter system with many steps, often expensive and inefficient. And even with a system of barter, it was not always possible to obtain needed supplies, particularly replacement parts.

In contrast to European factories, it is always striking to note how many women work in Russian factories, sometimes undertaking work that is quite heavy. As Marc Wurtz observed: "Here there's a woman told to lubricate some equipment with her oil can (her little dog in her arms), there a crane driver working on board the monster, down below again a woman domesticating her pneumatic drill … equality of women demonstrated by the facts! But I ought to admit that beyond the toasts and the frequent libations was the fact of the masculine 'tribe'."

From Gornosavodsk we went on to Neviansk, driving through a very heavy winter snowfall set among the endless fields and hilly forests of the Urals. Traveling for hours through such countryside, devoid of human life, we became truly aware of the dimensions of this enormous country (almost twice the size of USA). The only signs of life were occasional trucks traveling towards us. Our driver sped over the road at more than one hundred kilometers per hour. There were no other people and the road was completely covered with ice. Under such circumstances, it was scary to think what would have happened if our car had died in this icy wilderness or if it had started to skid. After a while, our two experienced drivers asked us to help them put snow chains on the tires, as we were about to enter hilly country, the highest rise challenging, though reaching no more than a hundred meters (100 yards) in height. Somewhere in this wintry forlorn wilderness, we crossed the boundary between the European and Asiatic continents, marked by a sign. After we had been traveling for several hours, there appeared a colony of flat-roofed buildings, somewhat set back from the road and fenced in by a double stockade two meters (6.5 feet) high, surrounded by barbed wire. This place, with clearly more than a thousand residents, appears on no maps and has only a code-number, not a name. Our colleagues from Alfa Cement explained that this place is one of the secret sites where military research and development takes place.

Somewhat numb with cold and from the frantic dash through the countryside, we reached, after a few hours, the cement work Neviansk. It does not belong to the Alfa-Cement group, but because it lies on our route and our companions are friendly with the managers, we make a courtesy call. After a brief tour of the factory, we move on to the important part of our visit, the luncheon. The director of the factory serves us an opulent feast in the strangely aesthetic, isolated setting of birch trees laden with snow. Hour after hour we are served new dishes and little tidbits. There is no stinting with the vodka, which flows generously and accompanies every toast. None of us are spared from giving a fine toast and from energetically warming ourselves up with vodka in the under-heated hut. The closer one sits to the director, the more one must keep pace with the energetic rhythm of his alcohol consumption. Marc Wurtz has the worst of it, for as the senior member of our delegation, protocol demands that he sit directly next to the host. Lower down the table, without being unpleasantly conspicuous, the remaining members of our delegation can spare themselves the excesses of vodka, only half emptying the glass after each toast. The director talks up a storm, scarcely able to stop after a few glasses. With each toast he gets louder and jollier until, after a few hours, much to our amazement, he stops abruptly and, in a soft, almost tearful voice, drinks a final toast to our continued safe journey, followed by a pious and reverent call for a minute of silence. The meal then loses momentum and we are able to travel on. We are not at all sorry for the Russian revelry to end, chilled to our bones and well past our saturation point, mindful of the long journey that still lies ahead. We leave the hut shortly before dark and travel through the night to Yekaterinburg. The next morning, somewhat exhausted, we reach this city, forty kilometers east of the imaginary line dividing Europe and Asia, the place where the last czar, Nicholas II, and his family were executed by the Bolsheviks in 1918.

After our early-morning arrival, we relax for a couple of hours in the hotel before we move on to Nishni Tagel. Here, too, there had been in Soviet times a large gulag near the city, a prison camp with sometimes as many as forty-three thousand prisoners. Alfa Cement owns a small part of this grinding mill, which stands in the middle of the city. The factory has not been in use for a long time and is in miserable condition. This ruin, and its director who is not quite sober when he greets us, are in a terminal condition. We spend little time on this hopeless case and soon travel on to Suchoi Log. This factory is about three hours east of Yekaterinburg and specializes in cement for the oil industry. The oil fields of the Tyumen region are northeast of the city. Because it deals with a niche market, the oil customers are at least able to pay with cash, a great advantage at this time.

The director gives the appearance of being a capable manager, able to lead his factory successfully, in contrast to his colleagues in some other plants. Suchoi Log appears to be in a relatively good condition, similar to that of Gornosavodsk. We are housed in a simple flat-roofed building that belongs to the factory, a place surrounded by endless snow-covered fields and woods. By now it is Saturday, and we indulge in recuperating in the work's *banya* (sauna). The sauna stands to the side of the factory, in the woods, and is a simple wooden house. Several times we warm ourselves up in the banya, then cool ourselves off in the snow. In between, we are refreshed with vodka and some food. A visit to a banya is always a relief after long cold days in a factory and in poorly heated offices. Supper with the director is as extravagant as everywhere in Russia, but happily does not finish with the excesses of the last dinner, perhaps because this director proved to be a sober host and we, presumably, showed signs of having no more energy for great feasts, apparent after our strenuous past few days.

The next Sunday morning brought us another pleasant experience. We were not leaving until the afternoon and, therefore, had some time in the morning for a tour through Russia's snow-covered landscape. The place where we were staying had the equipment we needed to make this expedition.

In the afternoon we traveled on to the airport at Yekaterinburg. From there we flew to Saratov, on the Volga in Southwest Russia.

Flights within Russia are always a peculiar experience. Generally speaking, modern planes are reserved in Russia for international flights, so very old machines are usually used for domestic flights. The musty, worn-out seats are of great age, as are the torn wall coverings, the carpets full of holes, and waste containers that cannot be closed. Water drips from the ceiling into the passenger compartment. The runways are always covered with snow and ice in winter, and I have never observed a plane being de-iced before takeoff. Interaction with the passengers usually leaves much to be desired. Passengers are regularly sent out to the field in temperatures under minus fifteen degrees Celsius (5 F), where they must wait for many minutes in the bitter cold before the plane is opened. The subsequent in-flight service is usually just as frosty. The flight attendants treat the passengers gruffly and angrily; the most they do is offer a cup of tea and a piece of candy. With the old Antonov propeller machines, no passenger can move after landing until the pilot leaves the cockpit, walks through the cabin, and leaves by the back exit before anyone else.

Saratov lies across from Engels, west of the Volga. The city was founded in 1590 as a fortress for the czar and has approximately 830,000 inhabitants. On the second day of our visit we toured, with Marc Wurtz and the plant director, the ruins of the once-great city, Ukek, about ten kilometers south of Saratov. Marco Polo mentions this city in the report of his travels. The tribes of the Golden Hoard, belonging to the Mongolian empire in Eastern Europe and Western Siberia, ruled the entire Volga-Don Region between the Caspian Sea and Ukek in the thirteenth and fourteenth centuries. The seat of government of the Mongolian-Turkish ruler was Berke-Sarai (Astrakan) on the Volga. The khans of the Golden

Hoard ruled Russia from 1240 to 1480, which was injurious to the economic position of Russia in Europe. The khans insisted on the division of Russia into meaningless dukedoms and therefore undertook repeated military campaigns. Czar Ivan III stopped payment of tribute to the Golden Hoard and ended the two hundred and fifty year foreign domination of the Tartar-Mongolians.

Central Saratov lies close to the banks of the Volga, 3,530 kilometers ( 2190 miles) long, which here, is about three kilometers (1,8 miles) wide. The Volga is the longest river in Europe and contains the most water. Catherine the Great settled the so-called Volga-Germans in the Saratov region. They were supposed to bring to Russia the more productive German agricultural methods. In this area there are numerous ethnic Germans, some still speaking German. Over the centuries they became completely assimilated, and not even communism resisted their agricultural methods, which were perhaps more efficient at the time. Today the whole region is just as Russian as the rest of the country.

Two hours from Saratov is the small city Volsk with its cement work, lying directly on the impressive Volga. The factory has several loading docks from which they can transport the cement by ship far to the north and to the south. To be sure, the Volga begins to freeze over in November and not until months later, about the beginning to the middle of April, does the snow begin to melt and the ice begin to break up.

Here the pace of life seems to be set by the easy flow of the Volga. The factory, impressively large, has an old and a new section. We do not often see the factory director. He appears to have gained this position principally through party politics and does not seem to understand much about producing cement. Although the factory is logistically well situated and possesses excellent raw material and the installation is well thought out, conditions are of less than average quality. Alfa Cement will have much to improve here and will also have to make personnel decisions involving the transfer of ownership.

With this factory we end our observation tour and fly back to Moscow from Saratov. When we land, we see, for the first time, a runway being de-iced, and by a most peculiar new method: hot air is blown on to the runway with the reactor of an airplane, brought across in a truck. Under the enormous pressure and the heat, the ice on the runway breaks up and flies through the air in the form of powerful flat pieces of ice – a quite brachial, inefficient, and also dangerous way of clearing the field. In the terminal we learn that Marc Wurtz' suitcase, checked with ours in Saratov, has not arrived. An energetic reclamation effort helps us to find the suitcase, thankfully in good condition, in one of the offices.

Judged by western standards and even by the standards at the time of border countries such as Chechnya and Hungary, the conditions in the Russian cement industry in general and in the plants we visited on this trip in particular were quite shocking: massive excess capacity, outmoded technology, plants of decreasing efficiency, decreasing demand, very low prices for the cement (twenty to thirty US dollars per ton), and inadequate liquidity, barely enough to pay wages. We were, nonetheless, convinced that it was merely a question of time until the Russian economy recovered, the cement market expanded, and the plants made money and could again invest in improvements. The first signs of recovery were indeed already visible in Moscow (as described above). In retrospect, this prediction was confirmed. The demand for cement and employment at the plants increased greatly, the price of cement climbed to over one hundred US dollars (per ton), and the industry gradually found its way back to making a profit and, through massive investments, modernized the plants. But to profit from these changes, it was both necessary and justified to take advantage of the uncertainties and risks of that era, for only at that early time were these advantageous positions available in the cement industry. A few years later the Russian market had been divided up, and all of the plants had been bought up.

## Chapter 9

## POVERTY AND INFLATION IN RUSSIA

In Moscow, Dominik and I saw many poor people trying to sell vegetables or old household goods. Additionally, there were also quite a few beggars. Our visits to various factories revealed a rural population living in poverty, within villages and small towns, on a par with those found in third world countries. Before privatization, older people at least had a modest pension. But the huge inflation of the post-Soviet era meant that the pensions paid for little more than a sandwich, and, as no work was available, life became very hard for the majority of the population.

The following text, appearing in Time Magazine on 24 October, 1994, furnishes a context for evaluating the Russian economy:

*"Moscow had recently been touting distinct signs of improved economic performance: inflation had slowed from a monthly rate of 25% last year to 4%, and the much battered ruble had been holding steady for about a month and had become something of a hard currency again in most of the former Soviet republics.*

*Then last week the ruble, which had begun to slip in September, nosedived within three hours of panicky trading, from 3081 to the dollar to 3900, as money dealers rushed to rid themselves of the currency. Ordinary folk joined the traders in bailing out, queuing up in front of street-corner exchange offices to offer bundles of rubles for dollars or deutsche marks. Shopkeepers shuttered their premises to mark up prices on par with the currency slump, and lines formed at gas stations as motorists tried to fill up their tanks before prices rose. By nightfall the ruble had lost 25% of its value – the largest single decline since free-floating exchange rates were introduced in 1992.*

*President Boris Yeltsin, calling the currency crash 'a threat to our national security,' fired acting Finance Minister Sergei Dubinin, a critic of easing monetary policy, and asked parliament to dismiss central bank chairman Victor Gerashenko – who resigned, but only after a personal meeting with Yeltsin. Considered by many an obstacle to reform, Gerashenko had balked at spending scarce hard-currency reserves to prop up the ruble as it went into free fall.*

*The following day after the central bank intervened, the ruble rebounded, and by week's end had climbed back to 2988 to the dollar. To some extent the panic-fueled plunge reflected the gap between the Yeltsin government's 'promise' of radical economic reform and 'its (actual) performance,' as well as its persistence in printing rubles to subsidize ailing state-controlled industries and farms.*

*In the next few weeks parliament must still consider the fate of Geraskenko and vote on the economic stewardship of Prime Minister Victor Chernomyrdin. In the meantime, the Russian public has already made its views known: as of last week, half the population is thought to be holding savings in U. S. dollars rather than rubles."*

Yeltsin had promised a rapid economic recovery. In an article entitled, "Another World," Roman Berger, Moscow correspondent for the Daily Report from 1991 to 2001, reports that in fact no economic recovery had taken place, but instead a decline which impoverished at least one third of the population. For months no wages, pensions, or salaries had been paid. The Russian economy functioned solely by bartering. Yeltsin was under pressure from the International Monetary Fund and other creditors and ruled only by decrees.

Unemployment and poverty are today still the lot of many people in Russia. About one third of the population still must make do with incomes under the minimum required for existence. While Moscow began to experience a boom in the nineteen nineties, poverty threatened many rural districts.

According to a 2001 report of the World Bank, too much attention has been paid to the macro-economic aspect in Russia. Russia's current malaise, it states, must be understood by looking at "specific cultural and historical burdens" of this country, to which the reform politics have paid too little attention. These "historical burdens" include a history of one thousand years of despots and seventy years of communism. The report says 2001 is not the "end of history."

## Chapter 10

## APPLICATION TO THE HOLDERBANK EXECUTIVE COMMITEE FOR A MANDATE TO NEGOTIATE A PARTNERSHIP WITH ALFA CEMENT, DECEMBER, 1993

I still remember that, in December 1993, Tres Pestalozzi had made a proposal to the Executive Committee. As far as I know, he explained, among other things, that Holderbank offered the possibility of entering into the Russian market with a successful partner. The great uncertainties – political, economic, and legal – would call for unconventional approaches (venture capital), making quite impossible at that time a standard feasibility study.

Tres worked on the assumption that the economic possibilities in Russia (raw material, energy, and so on) were positive. He seems also to have supposed it to be evident that with privatization a foreign investor would scarcely be able to become involved on his own but would have to acquire packets from private investment funds through the laborious purchase of vouchers that individual citizens had put together. He must also have mentioned that shares were purchased by arrangement with a holding company (Alfa Cement), a subsidiary of the Alfa Bank Investment Fund and a prominent cement manager. They attempted to purchase shares in all the plants they considered to be of interest. Aside from the state, these shares were mostly held by employees and, in greater amounts, by management.

At that time it was possible for Holderbank to participate in this holding arrangement by means of an increase in capital spending. The holding arrangement included the entire Russian cement industry, with fifty-one factories, employing an estimated fifty thousand workers and an annual capacity of eighty million tons of cement, at twenty-three percent. It had been decided at that time that an increase in capital from the Holderbank should be used to acquire more shares in the cement factories in question rather than, for instance, to modernize the plants. We were told that nineteen percent of the Holderbank in this holding arrangement (no IAS consolidation) would cost about seven million US dollars (with right of first refusal). At the time, the nineteen percent was the equivalent of owning a 3.2 million ton capacity.

To my great relief, as well as to Dominik's, Tres actually did get a mandate to negotiate entrance into a partnership (joint venture) with Alfa Cement on the basis of the proposed investment of a maximum of seven million US dollars, which in December 1993 was equivalent for Alfa Cement to about thirty-six million US dollars. The bold agreement to this on the part of the Executive Committee of Holderbank was not to be taken for granted, as the Russian economy in 1993 was in a decline which in that year ended in a decrease of about fifteen percent of the gross national product. Because of the liberal monetary policy, hyperinflation grew to a catastrophic nine hundred percent! A small ray of hope was to be seen in the balance of trade which, thanks to exports of energy, ended with a positive balance of ten billion US dollars. We knew that, among other things, ABB Ltd. (a Swiss energy and automation company) was already active in Russia with eleven financial participations, Coca Cola was planning on building a new factory near St. Petersburg for thirty million US dollars, and Phillip Morris, for sixty million US dollars, had acquired the majority of shares in a cigarette factory in Krasnodar.

Our studies showed that as a result of the great increase in the costs of energy and personnel, cement prices had risen, since the late 1980's to September 1993, on average, from two and a half US dollars per ton to over twenty US dollars per ton (bag); the specific increases were: Novorossiysk, twenty-one US dollars per ton; Zhigulevsk, twenty-five US dollars per ton, and in Moscow, the then remarkable price of thirty-five US dollars per ton. In 1989, cement had been customarily transported an average of 492 kilometers (306 miles).

It was clear to all of us that the Russian cement industry was in great need of significant improvements in plant technology. The factories, usually part of construction material combines, were generally run in a patriarchal style and were poorly maintained.

## Chapter 11

## FROM MOSCOW TO PERM AND THEN ON TO GORNOSAVODSK
JANUARY, 1994

On this trip with Tres, Dominik and I were accompanied by another representative from Holderbank. As it was usually cold in Moscow, I took the precaution of packing sensible winter clothing – a heavy coat of lambskin, high, well-lined boots, and a ski hat. After a peaceful supper in the Metropol Hotel and a refreshing overnight stay, we took a taxi ride of about thirty kilometers the next day to Domodedovo, one of several Moscow airports used mostly for domestic flights; today, it is a large international airport. Here no one understood either English or German. As none of us spoke Russian, we had to make our way as best we could. Only at the last minute were we seated in the right plane. To my surprise, there was no place to store either my flight bag or my colleague's luggage, so we had to put our bigger pieces of luggage in the narrow aisles. This won us critical looks from the unhelpful Russian stewardesses. Sometime after we took off, I found room for our hand luggage under the small, rather uncomfortable seats – which could be folded up, but still provided insufficient space below to accommodate a regular suitcase. Therefore, the flight bag had to be placed in the aisle of the plane. After a while, I came to realize why the other passengers had continued to don their coats, the men retaining their fur hats as well, the women their scarves. There was simply no place to store these items. Moreover, the temperature in the plane was barely ten degrees Celsius (50 degree F), warranting retention of protective clothing throughout the flight. With relief, after two hours, we learned that we would soon be landing in Perm. When the plane came to a stop, we immediately rose from our seats, a gesture disdained by the other passengers who remained seated, while expressing disapproval with *dirty looks.*

We did not know exactly what we had done wrong, but sensing we had violated some protocol, went back to our seats with our tail between our legs. It was quite a while after landing that the door to the cockpit opened and the captain and the co-pilot walked silently past the passengers to the exit. Only then did the Russian passengers begin to stir and head quietly toward the exit with their luggage, small pieces which, during the flight, had been stored properly under their seats.

Now we were in the Urals, a mountain range two thousand kilometers (1240 miles) – stretching from north to south. The city of Perm, on the river Kama, has a population of almost one million people. It is 1150 kilometers (930 miles) north-east of Moscow, as the crow flies. The infamous Prisoner Camp 207, for German war prisoners, is in Perm. After the war, there had been a large gulag housing twelve thousand prisoners who were exploited to build factories and roads. Because he had made critical comments about the dictator Josef Stalin, while serving in a military post, the famous Russian writer and dissident Alexander Solzhenitsyn was sentenced to spend several years in this gulag, a victim of the brutal prison system established by Stalin. Perm, until 1991, was off-limits to foreigners who lacked special permission to visit the site, it being the home of Russia's armaments industry; later, travel through Perm was made possible by the construction of the Trans-Siberian Railroad. Somewhat noteworthy is that a rural place near the city was the backdrop for an important scene from "Doctor Zhivago," a film based on a novel of the same name, by Boris Pasternak.

At ten o'clock at night, Kharif and four representatives of the Gornosavodsk Cement Company were waiting for us at the airport. It was snowing heavily, with an accumulation of new snow reaching upwards of thirty centimeters (12 inches). The temperature hovered around minus twenty degrees Celsius (–4 F), and it was clearly colder than in Moscow.

Now we were in the Urals, not far from the geographical boundary between Europe and Asia. The factory representatives had put two French Citroen vans at our disposal (evidently a present from our international competitors, Cement Francais) to take us directly to Gornosavodsk. One of the two vans was filled with provisions which served as reserves. After a brief but very friendly greeting, punctuated with many Russian embraces, we left Perm, immediately moving forward into the winter landscape that was blanketed under a heavy coating of snow. Soon there was nothing to see but forests dotted with birch trees; they seemed endless, while the road ahead was completely devoid of people – save for an occasional military vehicle. After more than an hour, we came to a barrier monitored by military guards equipped with machine guns. We came through this pass without difficulty and soon thereafter made a stop in this wilderness at the edge of the road. During our stop, we were offered warm coffee, sausages, bread, and pastries from the reserve van. We were very pleased at this refreshment break, as there had been virtually no food offered to us during our flight. It was still snowing and bitterly cold. I had visions of hungry wolves emerging from the woods, enticed by the aroma of the delicious rolls and sausages I was happily consuming. Might not these hungry wolves vie with me for these attractive staples! Man's deep-seated fear of wolves is well known. I did not know that, at that time, in Russia, it was legal to kill full grown wolves – be it by shooting, trapping, or poisoning them. Killing wolves, in fact, represented a profitable business, for the government was paying a substantial reward for every dead carcass. According to statistics, there are still about 280,000 wolves living in Russia, significantly fewer than in Canada. Following the brief pause to refresh ourselves, we drove another three hours through the seemingly endless birch forests, fortunately without seeing a wolf. From time to time we passed factories that were lit up. They were factories for processing oil or some sort of ore (bronze or platinum). Finally, though having driven through a snowstorm, we arrived in good shape; we had reached our destination – Gornosavodsk, a city of twelve thousand inhabitants. The city, about one hundred ninety kilometers northeast of Perm, is home to the cement factory of the same name, its most important industry. The next day we visited the factory, an enterprise which, like all Russian cement factories, was not quite up to western standards but, with substantial investments, could vastly improve its efficiency.

In Kharif's conference room we carried on our negotiations. The shares held by the Alfa Investment Fund were posted on the wall, and I photographed them.

» Gornosavodsk (2.8 million tons)   49%

» Volsk (2.6 million tons)   40%

» Sukhoi Log (2.7 million tons)   20%

» Novoross (3.9 million tons)   9%

» Zhigulevsk (1.8 million tons)   5%

» Topli (2.9 million tons)   3%

» Nevyansk (1 million tons)   1%

» Spassk (2.3 million tons)   0%

We established that Alfa Cement's portfolio contained not a single factory in the important region of Moscow. Thus our first priority had to be looking for such shares. The associates of the Alfa Investment Fund figured that the following additional shares could be purchased for US $7.80 million:

| | |
|---|---|
| » Gornosavodsk | +10% |
| » Volsk | +11% |
| » Sokhoi Log | +15% |
| » Neviansk | +20% |
| » Moscowa Regional Terminal | +09% |

For another additional US $7.50 million, still further shares could be purchased:

| | |
|---|---|
| » Sukhoi Log | +16% |
| » Novoros | +30% |
| » Neviansk | +5% |
| » Spassk | +5% |
| » Moscowa Regional terminal | +51% |

Meanwhile Tres Pestalozzi was quite delighted at the unique possibility of obtaining, rather cheaply, significant cement shares for Holderbank. Dominik and I, therefore, were confident that a reasonable deal ultimately could be made with the Alfa Investment Fund, with a real chance of gaining the approval of the Holderbank Executive Committee.

After we finished our negotiations with the Investment Fund, we were invited to see the workers' living quarters and the shops connected to them. They were grey five-story residential buildings with pre-fabricated concrete walls. The quality and construction standards were comparable to those one would find in a third-world country. This, by no means, was a *worker's paradise*. The apartments were tiny; but, perhaps as compensation for the cramped quarters, every family had a small dacha outside the city where, after the first of May, vegetables were planted and the children could run around. (There is a vacation on this date in Russia, a period set aside as a holiday.) In addition to the tour of the apartment buildings, we were also shown the social facilities for the workers which included a swimming pool, a sanatorium, a kindergarten, a canteen, and a sauna. These facilities were quite large, but were also constructed very poorly. Then we were invited to the sauna, designated for the top-management of the factory. It was made clear to us that we should go along with anything we might encounter at the sauna, even pretending we had looked forward to this moment all day. The top-level Russian managers enjoyed luxury services (for themselves and their guests) which included a warmed-up sauna (prepared in advance), clean towels and bathrobes, as well as snacks and various drinks served by a factory employee who offered it to guests before entering the sauna. But we Swiss, raised in a culture that prizes modesty as a virtue, could not quite follow the lead of our affable Russian hosts who, every fifteen minutes, urged us to pop up naked from the sauna and roll in a snow-heap located just five meters away. This particular activity, though it gave the Russians great pleasure, was not quite our style. As in all the other cement establishments that we visited later, virtually nothing seemed to have changed in the Gornosavodsk Cement Factory, despite the collapse of the Soviet Union. Everyone's daily life in the province went on as it had in the last years of the Soviet Union. The transition from the old to the new economic order proceeded much more visibly in Moscow than it had in the provinces.

In Perm, accompanied by Kharif, we visited one of his friends, the vice-governor of the region. Before we said goodbye at the airport, we saw the big Perm railway station, where many Russian passengers, clad in their warm winter clothes, were boarding and exiting the trains. This station was also a depot for the Trans-Siberian Railway.

When we arrived in Moscow, we took a little walk to stretch our legs, passing on our way the famous Manege, formerly a huge riding stable, about a ten-minute walk from the Metropol Hotel, the latter our place of residence during our visit. The Manege, a classical building encircled by Doric half-columns, was built by Czar Alexander the First to commemorate his victory over Napoleon's "*grande armée.*" As a tribute to the 1812 victory, a parade of two thousand soldiers had marched within its walls. But, on this particular afternoon, no parade was scheduled; instead, the venue would house a voucher auction – the particular enterprise-up-for-auction not widely known.

At the railway station in Perm beginning March 1994

In the Gornosadvosk plant end of February 1994: The author inspects the kiln oven.

## Chapter 12

## THE CONTRACT WITH ALFA CEMENT:
## FROM A ROUGH DRAFT TO A FINALIZED DEAL, READY FOR SIGNING
## JANUARY TO MAY 1994

Following is Dominik Wlodarczak's description of the evolutionary process in contract negotiations:

"Because of the uncertainties of the Russian legal system, we tried to insert as many assurances into the contract as possible. There followed, therefore, a period of intense negotiations regarding the conditions and requirements for developing a contract that would be acceptable to Holderbank. Conversations with Alexandrov were easy; he spoke fluent German because he had studied in Passau. Communication with Kharif's team, on the other hand, was more difficult, as no one on his team spoke good English. To overcome this problem, we had to use interpreters hired from outside at every meeting, a situation which was costly and which threatened the confidentiality of matters pertaining to the specifics of investments in the cement industry. To be sure, Anatoli, an independent professional translator, did an excellent job, appreciating the fine points of cultural differences between Russia and the West in these discussions. His professional experience as a translator had been at a high level, for he had even worked as a translator in talks between Gorbachov and Mrs. Thatcher. But Anatoli was not always available, and Alfa Cement looked for a new associate who would, among other things, be able to translate.

During one of our trips to Moscow with Tres, we saw, in the lobby of the Metropol Hotel, two Frenchmen from Ciment Francais accompanied by a Russian. About three weeks later, during our next visit to Moscow, Kharif introduced us to a certain Mr. Savitski, a new Alfa Cement employee who, from now on, was to translate all our conversations and to accompany us to all negotiations. He turned out to be the same person we had seen in the company of our competitor Ciment Francais. This distressed me greatly. My first reaction, as I had told Kharif in private, was to suspect some sort of conspiracy. He reassured us at once, explaining that Savitski had had contact with Ciment Francais as an embassy staff member in Paris, but would now be working solely for Alfa Cement. Moreover, Kharif could vouch for Savitski's integrity – as he had known and trusted this man for a long time.

Savitski spoke both very good English and French. Because of his experience as an embassy staff member in Paris, he was always able to present himself as a worldly-wise *"connoisseur."* On one occasion, for example, when we were eating with the Russian delegation at a good restaurant in Zurich, he gave the peppermill on the table back to the waiter and asked him to exchange it for a peppermill containing only red peppercorns, a supposed improvement in the type of seasoning appropriate for this meal. From the first, Savitski had belonged to Kharif's inner-circle and had participated in every session. His knowledge of both the western and Russian worlds was extremely helpful in building mutual understanding and trust between Holderbank and Alfa Cement. But we were never able to shake off our suspicion of the man, based on our knowledge that he had once been a representative of the KGB in the Paris embassy.

Our major accomplishment in our negotiations with our Russian partners is the text of the contract we developed with them, pounded out at the meetings held mostly with Alexandrov in Moscow. Part of the time that we spent at these meetings, we developed the text working directly at the computer. On other occasions we brooded with the lawyers over how certain conditions could best be integrated or formulated. Because Alexandrov subscribed to a daily regimen of intense body-building and regular calorie intake, he depended heavily on these aspects of his life-style to maintain his powers of concentration. Shamelessly, we tried to exploit his dependency on this unique life-style by scheduling negotiations frequently, lengthening them as much as possible and postponing breaks.

The early drafts that had grown out of these meetings were discussed with both Alfa Cement and Holderbank, later to be revised in larger groups. A delegation, familiar with the contract that had been developed in these recent negotiations with Alfa Cement and Holderbank now came to Switzerland in April 1994, headed by Kharif. We met in Zurich, in the conference rooms under the aegis of Dr. Anton E. Schrafl, vice-president of the board of directors of Holderbank Financière Glaris Ltd., the holding company of the Holderbank group. On this afternoon, the traditional Sechseläuten Procession was taking place, an annual spring festival held in Zürich, in the middle of April. The central character of the festival is the figure of Böög, an artificial snowman who symbolizes winter. About thirty-five hundred guild members participate, wearing their colorful costumes consisting of their national dress or familiar uniforms. Along with them various guests of honor – more than three hundred and fifty riders, around fifty wagons pulled by horses, and about thirty bands – march along the Bahnhofstrasse and the Limmatquai, heading towards the Sechsläutenplatz by the Bellevue. The guild members and guests of honor are showered from the spectators with flowers and kisses. At the end, the Böög is burned on a big funeral pyre. As he does every year, Toni Schrafl takes part in the procession as a member of the Constaffel Society. On this particular day, in the late afternoon, he dropped in the conference room unexpectedly, making his appearance in the midst of our negotiations with Alfa Cement. Like all the participants in the procession, he was dressed in a colorful medieval costume, crowned with a large floppy hat. As Derrick introduced Schrafl as the Vice-President of the Board of Holderbank, he reveled in the initial reaction of the Russians to this man – dressed as he was in such a bizarre costume. Their confusion about the costume was dispelled, however, when the context of his get-up was explained a little while later. From the explanation, they learned that all the fanfare of the parade and the strange apparel of its participants was a tribute to the Constaffel Society and the guilds, organizations whose guilds, in times past, had served not only a political and economic function, but a military function as well; and that Toni himself was a part of the Constaffel Society, and today is serving as a colonel in the Swiss army.

## Chapter 13

## A RETURN TO THE BONE-CHILLING CLIMATE OF THE URALS (AND HOW THIS HARSH CLIMATE HAD INFLUENCED HISTORY) FEBRUARY & MARCH 1994

In February and March 1994, Tres wanted to take another close look at the Gornosavodsk factory's technical condition as it bore on the planned signing of the contract with Alfa Cement. Because of my experience with the Russian winter, which is by no means over in March, I came to Moscow this time with proper winter clothes: a lambskin coat, a warm ski hat, and well-insulated boots. On this occasion, Dominik remained in Moscow to continue negotiations concerning certain details. The strenuous and unpleasant trip to Perm via a domestic flight, followed by a car trip through the endless snow-covered birch forests, was an effort actually worth making in light of the experiences that resulted after. The cold was more or less tolerable when we walked around the cement factory, periodically stationing ourselves close to the hot rotary furnaces. In the late afternoon, as our well-earned reward, there was the usual sauna routine – no thought of the penetrating cold there. The next morning we headed towards Perm in a Citroen van driven by the factory chauffeur, racing at a hundred kilometers an hour. The heater in the van was out of order. Fortunately I had the clothing described above in the boot of the car, but in spite of that, I was colder than I had ever been in my life and managed to repress all thought of the true danger of the ride. At the time of our departure from Moscow, the temperature was just minus twenty degrees Celsius (-4 F); in the Urals it was five degrees colder which meant a temperature of -13 F. Since the speed chosen by the driver seemed to me to be dangerous, I suggested, in jest, to Tres Pestalozzi that he take over the wheel for a while. Tres agreed with this suggestion and explained his plan to the driver. The car stopped and Tres took over the wheel, the driver now sitting in the passenger seat beside him. I took advantage of this short break to perform a one-minute Indian dance in order to warm myself up a bit. Surprisingly, unlike me, Tres never complained of the cold. He drove more slowly than the factory chauffeur, but had no experience navigating over the hazardous roads of the Urals, leaving me to continue pondering the dangers the road conditions represented, despite the change of drivers.

In the remaining time of the trip to Perm – at least three hours – I contemplated the effect of the Russian climate on the armies of Napoleon and Hitler, a factor that must have played a significant role in the losses they both suffered.

Napoleon's Russian campaign took place in 1812, during the reign of Czar Alexander I. The French emperor's entrance into Russia coincided with an atypical heat wave. Many soldiers and horses suffered heatstroke. This was followed at first by a mild winter, from the middle of October to the sixth of November, and on November 14, 1812, the French marched into Moscow, despite bloody losses in Borodino. But the city was already ablaze, set afire by the Russians themselves. The winter started in earnest on November 7, and on November 11 the temperature dropped suddenly to minus twenty-eight degrees Celsius. Many soldiers fell ill, and the troops were demoralized. On November 19, Napoleon ordered a retreat. By then two thirds of the Grande Armée were dead. Due to snow and ice, many soldiers and horses broke their legs. Reserves of clothing and medical supplies gave out. On November 21, surrounded by three Russian armies, the French army reached the east bank of the Berezina River, a branch of the Dnieper. Attempts at crossing the Berezina were stalled by ice and blown-up bridges. Only thirteen hundred men remained of an original eight thousand, grouped in four Swiss regiments belonging to the Merle Division. They had to secure the retreat of the French army over the Berezina. On the morning of November 28, the Swiss prepared for battle. Lacking ammunition, the Swiss resorted to attacking with bayonets, enabling the Legrand and Maison Divisions to regain the upper hand. After eight Swiss bayonet attacks, the Russians, who, having greater numbers up to that point which had given them the upper hand, now saw the tide of battle turn, preventing them from claiming a clear victory. Only three hundred Swiss showed up for the last call to arms. The "Berezina Song" has thus become the symbol of sacrifice. This song we sang sometimes in the Swiss military (Infantry) in the manoevers when we were dead tired.

Of an original 610,000 soldiers, more than two thirds died in the Russian campaign. Thus only one soldier in three survived the war. Another 160,000 French soldiers were imprisoned by the Russians until 1814.

On June 20, 1941, Hitler began his Blitzkrieg (Campaign Barbarossa), planned to be completed in nine to seventeen weeks. The main target was Moscow. The plan for a summer campaign did not take into account Napoleon's experience. Having the advantage of a surprise attack, the three German army groups advanced rapidly towards the east, in accordance with the Barbarossa Plan of attack. At the beginning of September, the army group Nord, having marched through the Baltic states via East Prussia, cut off the city of Leningrad (St. Petersburg) from all connections with land. Hitler wanted to starve the city, but despite a nine hundred day siege, the will of the entrapped citizens could not be broken. On September 9, 2011, the Neue Zurcher Zeitung reported that seventy years ago, on September 8, German and Finnish troops completed the encirclement of Leningrad, the Soviet Union's second-largest city. The city of three million was cut off from all supplies. This was the beginning of the 872-day blockade (1941–1944), one of the greatest crimes in modern history. The most common cause of death was starvation, but other causes were cold, shooting, and bombing. The death toll of civilians is estimated at 1.1. million. In a secret directive, No. 1a 160/41, dated September 26, 1941, Hitler declared that Leningrad was to be wiped off the face of the earth. After the conquest of Soviet Russia, he argued, the continued existence of this city would serve no purpose.

But as early as October 1941, the German troops heading for Moscow, slowed by the muddy soil, made little progress. After suffering many losses, they reached the outskirts of Moscow. The attack came almost to a standstill because of the autumn mud and the increased resistance of the Red Army. The second offensive of the German army also failed. On December 5, the Red Army launched a massive counterattack, leading Hitler, on January 15, 1942, to order his troops to retreat from the outskirts of Moscow. At the beginning of December, snow and icy temperatures brought the attack to a complete standstill. Because of their arrogant prediction of a Blitzkrieg (instant conquest), the majority of the German troops did not come prepared with winter clothes or sufficient armaments able to hold up for the long winter stay. The losses caused by the freezing weather outstripped the number of deaths that occurred in direct battle. By the end of 1941, the German army had losses that could scarcely be compensated; more than 220,000 dead and 620,000 wounded. By May 1945, about three and a half million German soldiers had lost their lives on the eastern front, thanks to the Nazi regime's insane lust for expansion. The Russian losses totaled about twenty million – fourteen million soldiers and six million civilians. By February 1942, a mere 1.1 million of the original 3.9 million soldiers of the Red Army who were imprisoned, remained alive. Packed into over-crowded camps fenced in by barbed wire, they were simply left to die of hunger or illness.

Despite the rapid German advance, the Soviets had, in 1941, most of their armaments in the Urals and sent them to safety in Siberia. In the battle of the winter of 1941–1942, with the Soviet offensive fortified by new troops, there began the German army's westward retreat, which was to continue for a number of years.

On trips from the Sheremetyevo Airport in Moscow, we occasionally saw the memorial, made of steel beams, showing the point outside Moscow reached by the German troops before they had to begin their ignominious retreat.

Fortunately the dangerous car trip from Gornosavodsk to Perm, fraught as it was with the hazards of travel in Russia's harsh winter landscape, was completed without incident. Flying out of Perm, we arrived in Moscow, grateful to be *intact*. This time our stay in Moscow was not at the Metropol, but rather at the National – a hotel equally accommodating and equally well-situated. Located at the intersection of Mokhovaya and Tverskaya, the hotel situates the visitor in an ideal location, across from the Kremlin and near St. Basil's Cathedral, the latter famous for its onion towers. We returned to this hotel on several trips to Moscow, taken later.

## Chapter 14

### "HOLDERBANK" – BODYGUARDS and a RENTED STRETCH-LIMOUSINE 1994

When the USSR collapsed and a free economy emerged, organized criminal groups began to take over Russia's economy – with many ex-KGB officers and veterans of the war in Afghanistan offering their skills to crime bosses.

After the press again started reporting the serial murders of Russian businessmen, Tres Pestalozzi began to fear that on our next trip to Russia we, too, would be Mafia targets. Thus all of us were alerted by the Alfa Bank managers of their concern for our safety. They used armored vehicles and bodyguards, changed cars regularly, and took a different route to work each day. As an additional precaution, Tres arranged guards for our time in Moscow through the safety advisors of Holderbank.

Upon our arrival in Moscow, we were picked up by four steeled body guards – suited up in bullet-proof vests. From then on and throughout the trip, we were not allowed out of their sight. The guards inspected the car thoroughly before we entered it, making sure no bombs had been placed underneath. During the night, they stood outside our hotel rooms. Paradoxically, the presence of the guards drew attention to us wherever we went. When we entered a restaurant with our bodyguards, everyone immediately took notice, speculating that we must be very important to warrant so much protection. In this respect, the whole exercise of protecting us was counter-productive. If someone had wanted to shoot us down, our guardian angels could not have stopped them. At best, they could have prevented our being kidnapped, but not our being murdered.

In autumn, 1994, we were once again in Moscow with Tres and were faced with a heavy program, including many meetings with Kharif, our lawyers, the International Finance Corporation (IFC) – an offshoot of the World Bank, and various official bodies. Dominik and I decided to rent a luxury car so as to give Tres as good an impression as possible of doing business in Russia. The only car available was an American stretch limousine (a restructured Lincoln Town Car) more than ten meters (11 yards) long, a model favored by the Mafia when carrying out their criminal activities. This car, which had darkened windows, was very comfortable. Between the spacious seats were little boxes containing various snacks and beverages. Once we got over our Swiss sense of thrift and started behaving more brashly, in the style of a Mafiosi or oligarchs, we had to laugh at ourselves, realizing that, at the very least, we should play the role of an important VIP, though still lacking the ultimate symbol of prestige – the blue light on the roof of the car.

There was a hopeless traffic jam in the middle of the city when we finished the last session. We wanted Savitzki to drive us to the airport, in time to board a plane that would get us back to Switzerland the same evening. Given the traffic, it seemed it would be impossible to get to the airport on time. Noticing our nervousness, Savitzki drove the big Alfa Bank car on to the sidewalk and zigzagged along about four hundred meters, without any regard to the pedestrians. Message conveyed by his outlandish behavior: Moscow pedestrians have no rights on either the zebra crossings or on the sidewalk. In this reckless fashion, Savitzki bypassed at least sixty cars, making it possible, in a reasonable amount of time, to reach one of the main roads, where the traffic moved more quickly. At the last minute, we made our flight back to Switzerland.

## Chapter 15

## SADKO – THE FIRST LUXURY SHOPPING CENTER IN MOSCOW (THREATENED AT THE OUTSET BY MAFIA EXTORTION)

Sadko is the name of a hero in a Russian saga of that name. It tells how Sadko becomes rich with the help of the King of the Sea and later becomes his captive at the bottom of the sea and is freed with the help of Saint Nicholas. Rimsky-Korsakov wrote an opera in seven scenes entitled Sadko.

Our Russian friends told us we should not fail to visit the first shopping center ever developed in Moscow, the Sadko Arcade. We would then see with our own eyes that Russia had entered a new era. We did not wait to be asked twice but took the first opportunity to visit this example of economic awakening in Russia. Only then did we learn that Sadko was a *joint* Russian-Swiss venture; one hundred percent ownership was not possible at that time. The principal shareholder was Hopf Service Incorporated (the Bon Appetit Group) in Zürich-Glattbrugg. Sadko was active in retail (food and other goods) and owned, in addition, seven high-end shops and nine restaurants, including a typical Swiss restaurant featuring raclette and fondue on the menu, the décor inspired by Swiss folklore.

When completed, the Sadko Arcade included nineteen shops: high-end fashion shops, supermarkets, confectioners, bakeries, and a butcher shop. The Sadko shopping center had its own warehouse and imported everything, using four hundred and fifty trucks. As there were few western-style shops and restaurants in 1993–1994, this shopping center was an absolute must for wealthy Russians. I remember shops with a very fancy inventory of children's toys – little cars and huge bears – that sold for thousands of American dollars.

Though Sadko grew rich, he found himself, one day, in the clutches of the King of the Sea. In the modern version of this Russian saga, a new twist is added: one day some men in dark suits appeared in the Sadko offices, laid a machine gun on the table, and for once did not demand the usual protection money. In a friendly but firm manner, they suggested a new deal: while the price of the shares should be made to rise immediately, somehow the Swiss portion was to remain the same in total value; this method of calculating the worth of the shares gave the Russians a clear majority of what, initially, purported to be a *joint* venture. To deal with this emergency, Sadko called upon St. Nicholas for help. The Swiss ambassador at the time, Dr. Johann Bucher, acting as St. Nicholas might have done, intervened skillfully with the Russian ministry, which immediately made use of the unorthodox remedies available to it. For a time, at least, a modern-day St. Nicholas was able to free Sadko from the brutal reality of transacting business in Mafiosi-riddled Russia.

# Chapter 16

## TOUGH NEGOTIATIONS

Dominik described our many rounds of negotiations with Alfa Cement as follows:

"Both Holderbank and Alfa Cement were tough negotiators, although there was from the beginning a good feeling between the two. The mutual trust that started with the first contact rose continually, and both sides basically wanted the deal to go through. More than once, we had to break off a meeting in order to emphasize our conditions or to resist new demands made suddenly by the other side; yet these challenges, complicated as they were, did not prevent negotiations from getting back on track.

In developing protective measures of strategic importance, we focused on the location of factories best suited to our investment concerns. Specifically, we insisted that Alfa Cement acquire a cement position in the vicinity of Moscow, the most important market place in Russia, for, as yet, they did not have any facilities in the area. We also insisted that they acquire the Spassk Factory, near Vladivostok, as the location affords relative ease in exporting cement by sea, throughout Asia. Most importantly, control of these factories provides the possibility of dealing in foreign currency, a great advantage given the absence of liquidity throughout the Russian economy. Yet, given the narrow window of opportunity for privatizing these two facilities, our concerns had to be addressed quickly. So Alfa Cement, using privatization vouchers, started to buy up shares in Shurovo, a company near Moscow.

Simply owning a plant in Shurovo was not enough to be successful in the Moscow cement market. All cement enterprises in the capital city were dominated by a single company, Stern Cement. Most production depended on this organization which had its own cement terminal in the city, along with rail and street logistics for distribution. At first we considered a cooperative arrangement with Stern Cement but, once in control of Shurovo, we contemplated the possibility of developing a distribution system of our own."

Dominik continued, "These thoughts suddenly took a turn in a definite direction without our doing anything. As soon as I arrived at the Metropol Hotel in Moscow and entered my room, the telephone rang. A representative of Stern Cement introduced himself in broken English and said he would like to see me. I found myself in a touchy situation. I had had, up to then, no contact with this organization and discovered that I was under surveillance from strangers; they knew exactly who I was and the exact day and time when I would arrive at a particular hotel in Moscow. Since I knew from the first who was involved, I agreed to meet, even though the incident seemed, at first, to be uncanny. We seemed to have survived certain intimidating business practices prevalent during Soviet times to which we Swiss were not accustomed.

After this audacious first contact, we had a number of conversations with Stern Cement. My partner in these talks, Juri, was the owner's son, who went to school in the USA and spoke good English. However, no practical results came of these talks because Stern Cement was not ready to enter into a true partnership or to give shares to Alfa Cement. Also, Kharif, who was well acquainted with the Stern family and their enterprises, wanted to construct Alfa Cement's own distribution system in Moscow. Apparently, some mistrust existed between these two Jewish businessmen, Kharif and Stern. Within this context, practical talks about actual operations in the Moscow market could not go forward."

## Chapter 17

THE CONTRACT BETWEEN HOLDERBANK AND ALFA CEMENT
MAY 1994

By May 24, 1994, we had reached a point in our negotiations when we declared our readiness to present a contract acceptable to both sides. Dominik and I watched breathlessly as, in the presence of the Russian delegation, and at the office of Chadbourne and Park, Tres Pestalozzi signed the contract. Some sixteen months had passed since Alexandrov, in the beginning of 1993, had visited Holderbank and made his first contact with us; at the time, he was the Russian representative of Alfa Cement, subsequently renamed the Alfa Investment Fund. In between, there had been many visits from both sides, sometimes laborious and strenuous, held at factories in far-flung regions of Russia, or convened in Moscow, Holderbank, and Zürich, characterized by complicated negotiations. Despite the hardships suffered, Dominik and I remained fascinated with the project and with the great unknowns of Russia – its land and its people.

Through the contract with Alfa Cement, Holderbank, for twenty million US dollars (at that time, the sum of 20 million US dollars, was approximate equivalent of 30 million Swiss francs), received a nineteen percent share in the consolidated capacity of all the cement factories participating in Alpha Cement. Though this capacity was assessed at twelve million tons of cement, true for the individual factories who held only a minority of shares, an interest in the *consolidated* capacity promised much more – i.e., a capacity of more than twenty million tons.

This contract also included the following investment policy, once Holderbank was included:

"Glenfed (Glenfed Investment S.A., Panama, and 'Holderbank' Financiers Glaris Ltd., collectively called Glenfed) will join Alfa Cement as a new and equal partner. The capital increase which will result from Glenfed participation will be used to acquire participations (shares) in new cement and cement-related companies in Russia or to increase existing shareholdings. Such acquisitions will be made directly from the sellers at market prices and no fees will be charged to any Alfa Cement shareholders.

A number of acquisition targets in which the Glenfed contribution will be invested have been identified by all parties. Those targets were listed in an Appendix of the contract.

None of the Glenfed contributions will be invested or used for upgrading or modernization of the Alfa cement plants …"

After the signing of the contract in May 1994 in Moscow. Left: S. Kharif and right A. Pestalozzi.

## Chapter 18

PRIVATIZATION AND PLEDGE AUCTIONS (LOANS FOR SHARES) 1995 TO 1999

Only through newspapers and conversations did Dominik and I learn about a second round of negotiations involving privatization. Since this second round of negotiations had no further direct effect on the cement shares already acquired, we were not confronted in detail with the specifics of these meetings.

The background of the renewed interest in privatization involved the fiscal crisis in Russia that was extremely acute in 1995 and had to be resolved by Boris Yeltsin and the reformers. The country had enormous problems with the budget, as expenditures greatly exceeded income. In March 1995, the Oneksimbank, headed by Vladimir Potanin, proposed a solution to President Yeltsin. Through an agreement with the heads of other powerful banks, such as Menatep, Inkombank, Imperial and Stolichny, banks could make a large loan to the Russian government for one year. As security, the banks would hold and manage some of the stocks of twenty-nine large Russian firms in trust for the government. The majority of these stocks from state firms were oil and mineral companies, the cream of the state companies. The shares pledged by the government were to be auctioned off in an open and competitive auction – known as a 'pledge' auction – and distributed among the banks as security. The money received at the auction was to be "lent" to the Russian government. If by the end of the year for which the loan was stipulated, September 1, 1996, after the projected presidential election in the summer, the Russian government was to decide not to pay back the loan to the banks, the packet of shares would be transferred to the winners of the auction and would become their property. President Yeltsin authorized this plan in a decree (No. 889), and the banks were authorized to organize the pledge auction.

But the banks, in advance, had agreed among themselves which banks would bid on particular shares. Leonid Nivzlin, a business partner of the Menatep Bank, which was headed by Mikhail Khodorkovsky, explained that the banks settled among themselves who would get what. They further agreed that they would not compete at the auction. As the auctions were public, it was always possible that an outsider would show up. But the reformer Alfred Kokh saw to it that, for "technical reasons," these new bidders (financial institutions) were excluded from seven auctions involving packets of shares. The ones in question included, among others, the highly lucrative oil companies (Lukoil, Sidanko, Yukos, and Sibneft) and the most important mineral and metal firms (Norilsk Nickel). In all, twelve pledge auctions were held. The most valuable prize, Norilsk Nickel, fell into the hands of Potanin, the initiator of the pledge auctions. Norilsk Nickel is the world's largest producer of nickel and palladium. According to the Neue Züricher Zeitung (May 11, 2011), its market capitalization is some 34.7 billion US dollars. This firm is said somewhat later to have brought Potanin's financial and industrial empire one hundred million US dollars a month. Michail Khodorovsky secured through the auctions the earth oil company Yukos. "Finding gaps in the law and making use of them, completely or partially – that was the greatest intellectual pleasure in this business," Khodorovsky later told the well-known author Ludmila Ulitskaya, finding the loopholes in the law represented the most satisfying and challenging aspects of the business negotiations of that time (Neue Zurcher Zeitung, November 11, 2011).

The government got only eight hundred million US dollars as a loan from the auction. This type of unbridled capitalism had already existed, namely in America, where the Rockefellers or the Vanderbilts acquired their huge assets in questionable ways. In the second half of the nineteenth century new industries came into being in America. The so-called robber barons climbed to the greatest heights of the economy. They used extremely unscrupulous methods: shareholders were given unfair advantages, quotations of shares were arbitrarily manipulated, politicians were bribed on a grand scale, and competitors were excluded by questionable means. Over the course of this process, enormous empires grew rapidly, for economic regulations barely existed and the most unscrupulous manipulators took over, in the style of the Wild West. Large trusts were set up in many spheres, controlling and monopolizing ever greater portions of particular industries, at the cost of the clients.

## Chapter 19

## THE RISE OF THE OLIGARCHS
## 1995 TO 1997

I came to fully understand the pledge auctions, the rise of the oligarchs, and the details of the various phases of privatization only when I had the opportunity to read a case-study as a basis for a course at the Harvard Business School entitled, "Russia, the End of a Time of Troubles?," held on May 24, 2001 (Rev. 9–701–076). Dominik and I were eye witnesses to the privatization in the cement industry that took place between 1993 and 1994 and to the very special atmosphere in Russia during that period. Up until 1998, I myself traveled to Russia a number of times each year. But despite many trips to Russia, we failed to grasp in detail the greater connections in this phase of privatization. It is worthwhile to examine briefly this entirely different round of privatization, during which the rich became much richer.

In the mid-nineties, the Russians began to describe a few powerful businessmen as oligarchs. This description referred to the huge fortunes that were rapidly acquired and the resulting political influence. The Russian word, "prikhvatit", means to grasp or to grab. The Russians changed the meaning of the word "privatizatsiia," from "privatizing" to "grabization," a play on words. Many Russians believe that the oligarchs did more than just *grabbing* to acquire their riches.

Yeltsin hit a low point before the presidential election in the summer of 1996 and received a mere five percent approval. At the same time, the popularity of Gennady Zyuganov, the head of the communist party, grew with the economic crisis. At the beginning of 1996, most political analysts believed that Zyuganov would almost certainly win the election. Almost all Swiss newspapers agreed that Yeltsin would lose the election and that Russia would fall back into communism.

In February 1996 my former Holderbank boss, Dr. Anton Schrafl, invited me to a meeting of potential western investors at the World Economic Forum (WEF) in Davos, attended by Russian politicians and leading economists. The Russian brain-storming took place in the Hotel Derby "Drusa" on Saturday, February 4, 1996. As Toni and I arrived ahead of time, we were able to hold a few places at the table where the Russian delegation was having a late supper. The room was already pretty full when Gennady Zyuganov and two companions entered the bar. I went up to them and invited them to our table. Since 1993, Zyuganov had been the head of the Communist Party of the Russian Federation, a member of the Duma, and likewise a member of the Council of Europe. He was Yeltsin's most dangerous opponent in the presidential election. Zyuganov, clearly intelligent, seemed self-confident and had a loud voice, appearing to be a man of the people. To be sure, his blustery manner and muscular figure gave me goose-flesh. I shuddered at the thought that this communist leader was very likely to become the next president of Russia and turn back the wheel of history. Toni and I spoke with him about the cement shares held by Holderbank in Russia and our plans to modernize the plants and educate the cadres and the staff. Zyuganov seemed satisfied with our presentation. When we made our way back to our hotel, through deep snow, after supper, Toni and I agreed that if our neighbor at the table were actually to win the election and Russia again to become communist, the new communist Russian president would at least not be hostile from the outset to the Holderbank cement shares in Russia.

In the American "New Perspectives Quarterly" (February 1996), I read the following about the WEF, in Davos, in an article by Nathan Gardels:

"When Russian Communist Party leader Gennady Zyuganov could not answer Senator Bill Bradley's direct questions about guarantees on privatization if his party regained power, he lost whatever sympathy he may have had from the audience of western corporate leaders and financiers gathered in the Plenary Hall. Instead, Zyuganov talked about 'pillage' of the national patrimony, wages and pensions gone unpaid and unemployment levels in Russia as high as America's during the Great Depression. In contrast, Grigory Yavlinsky, a democratic reformist and former Soviet Deputy Prime Minster (founder and leader of the Yabloko Bloc in the Russian Parliament), pleased the gathering with soothing assurances on private property and his sophisticated analysis calling for increased productivity as the best way to pay for the social state.

Yavlinsky won hands down in Davos; Zyuganov will win in Moscow ...

'Successful privatization takes time', said Russian Communist Party leader Gennady Zyuganov and so far in Russia, privatization has not produced the desired results; therefore privatization 'has to be looked into.'

Even Grigory Yavlinsky admits that the financial stabilization program of the market reformers in Russia was so successfully implemented that it fathered the reaction we see now. The operation was a success, Yavlinsky says, but the patient is dead."

In a WEF communique of February 4, 1996, concerning a discussion on the theme, Russian politics and economics, the following appears under the title, "Russian Communist Party Leader Attacks Yeltsin Reform as National Disaster." "Unrealistic government policies had caused a situation in Russia where the economic situation is going from 'worse to worse' with production and investment dramatically down, the social system in disarray, and the legal and tax system chaotic, Gennady Zyuganov told a packed session. If elected to the presidency in Russia's election in June, he would like to introduce a mixed state and private market system 'where everyone is able to function' and foreign investors face predictable business conditions. Today, he claimed, Russia is economically drained by the mafia and corrupt bureaucrats. Declaring that he favors a stable, multi-party political system, Zyuganov said that he supports laws which are up to international standards, reasonable economic competition and open politics. He wants a government which fulfills its commitments, and does 'simple things like pay people's wages.'"

I learned from the list of participants in the Russian evening brainstorming session in the Hotel Derby that the following known personalities, among others, were present on February 4, 1996: Anatoly Chubais (Chairman of the Board, Russian Privatization Centre), Francis Fukuyama (Senior Researcher, Rand Corporation, USA), Andrei Kokoshin (Deputy Minister of Defense of Russia), Yuri Luzhkov (Mayor of Moscow), Vladimir Putin (First Deputy Mayor of St. Petersburg), Yevgeny Yasin (Minister of Economics of Russia), and Jeffrey Sachs (Harvard University, USA).

Let me mention something else that happened. On Monday, February 6, 1996 – that is, after participating in the Russian brainstorming of February 4 at the WEF meeting in Davos – when I was sitting beside Tres Pestalozzi in the totally booked Swissair plane heading for Moscow, I noticed Grigory Yavlinsky sitting in the row across from us and trying repeatedly, without success, to stow his heavy winter coat. As the flight attendants gave him no help, I got up and took his coat, which I put in a closet by the entrance of the plane. Tres commented laconically that this friendly gesture might one day pay off.

In an essay entitled, "After Yeltsin, Who?" (New York Times, January 30, 1995), and a year earlier William Safire wrote, "In the most recent poll of Russian voters, Grigory Yavlinsky – his name means 'The man who appears' – now draws more support for the position of President than Boris Yeltsin. That says less about the growing strength of the 42-year-old economist from Lvov, head of a reformist bloc in Parliament, than it does about a collapse of public backing for the President who ordered 60,000 troops to wipe out a few thousand secessionists in Chechnya. The 'conqueror of Grozny' is now down to single-digit support, along with his Prime Minister, Victor Chernomyrdin. Democratic reformers, along with legions of mothers of young soldiers, have abandoned Yeltsin because he chose war over prolonged negotiations. Nationalists and Communists are furious because he revealed the ineptitude of the army and brought further shame on the nation …"

In 1996, the oligarchs were much more worried than we were about Zyuganov possibly becoming the president. They feared he would end the Russian experiment with a market economy and democracy. In January, 1996, polls showed Zyuganov clearly leading, while Yeltsin was in only the fifth position; just eight percent of the public would support him in another election. Given this situation, it was feared that the communist leader would not honor the settlements from the pledge auctions. In that case, the oligarchs would lose a large part of their possessions, not to mention their political influence.

At the above-mentioned February, 1996, WEF meeting in Davos, the most powerful business people in Russia, along with Anatoly Chubais, vowed to support President Yeltsin in his campaign, with all available means. Chubais was to organize Yeltsin's re-election campaign, to which the oligarchs pledged massive financial support. This Davos pact included Boris Berezovsky, Vladimir Gussinsky, Mikhail Khodorkosky, Vladimir Potanin, and Alexander Smolensky – that is, everyone who participated in the pledge auction. But even the two critics of the pledge auction, Mikhail Fridman and Piotr Aven from the Alfa Bank, joined in, as they were convinced that Zyuganov posed a serious threat. This group donated their media influence to Yeltsin's campaign: television, radio, and newspapers. They also contributed their regional contacts and, of course, a lot of money. The money involved came to three-figured millions of US dollars.

As we know, Yeltsin finally won the election, held on June 16, 1996, with just thirty-five percent of the votes. His opponent, Zyuganov, was in second place, with thirty-two percent of the votes. In August, the reelected president Yeltsin named Vladimir Potanin, from the Oneksim Bank, the Deputy Prime Minister. In September, the Yeltsin Administration decided not to repay the money loaned from the pledge auction. Thus the property of the state packets of shares of the important firms dealing with natural resources was transferred to the banks, which up to that point were only holding them as collateral. The well-to-do businessmen became fabulously wealthy and entered into history as oligarchs.

As an example, take Vladimir Gussinky, founder of the Most Bank and the station NTW. According to Gisela Tobler's book, "Russians are Different," about the experiences of Karl Eckstein, Gussinsky worked in crooked ways, among other things, deceiving a firm in Singapore regarding shares. Gussinsky, she says, was closely allied with the mayor of Moscow, Juri Luschkov, so it is probably no coincidence that almost all state holdings in Moscow were administered by Gussinsky's Most Bank. He enjoyed numerous privileges, and he rode through Moscow with a blue light atop his car, like a high state official. According to the Neue Zurcher Zeitung (November 20, 2011), he had, on that Sunday, to sell his shares in Most Bank because he had fallen out of favor with President Putin. In order to escape a warrant for his arrest, he headed for Spain in 2001. Today Gussinsky lives in Israel, where he works as the majority shareholder of the Russian-language television station, RTVi.

In an article in "Der Sonntag" (April 12, 2011), the following appeared under the headline, "Potanin skimmed off millions." "The oligarch is said to have moved seven hundred ninety million francs from Hyposwiss, a branch of the St. Gallen Cantonal Bank, to Cyprus. A charge was levied against him by Oleg Deripaska, also a billionaire oligarch. Deripaska accuses Potanin of withdrawing unconstitutionally one million francs from the far larger Norilski Nikel company (Mining and Metallurical), in which both had shares. Hyposwiss is said to have helped him do this. Did Potanin do this in hopes of bringing his money to safety, fearing it would be blocked? According to an account of his total assets as of February, 2011, as reported in Der Sonntag, Potanin controlled extensive cash. His assets came to six hundred and eighty-five million francs. In March, dividends of ninety-one million francs were added to this, according to an e-mail to Hans Bodmer. With these total assets, the oligarch was living in high style. His expenses in February totaled more than twenty-seven million francs. Some of the larger items included expenses for his two super yachts Y-707 and Anastasia as well as for two gulfstream jets.

The renowned economic journalist Julia Latynia once lamented that there were no longer institutions in Russia, only personal connections (Gisela Tobler, "Russians are Different"). Above all, corruption is wide-spread among the economic elite, an elite cartel in which executive and high finance have bonded together and thus influence the political process. There are, to be sure, some boundaries to this connection, as seen in the case of Khodorkovsky. As the head of the giant oil concern Yukos, he was Russia's richest man until 2003. With his oil millions, he supported liberal opposition parties such as Jabloko and SPS, which displeased the Kremlin. Since 2003, Khodorkovsky has been sitting in prison. Forty percent of his Yukos shares were seized.

## Chapter 20

## A FIRST VISIT TO SHUROVO (SHUROVSKY TSEMENT) MARCH/APRIL, 1994

Since we found in our various interventions with Kharif and his associates that Alfa Cement had no shares in factories that could serve the Moscow area, Alfa Cement began to pick up the pace of purchasing vouchers from Shurovo. First they used money made available to them by Alfa Bank. After the contract between Holderbank and Alfa Cement was signed, in May, 1994, they used the money that Holderbank had paid as a partner of Alfa Cement. Ciments Lafarge, Holderbank's big French competitor, had already been able to buy shares in Voskresensk-Tsement, located just eighty kilometers south of Moscow.

On a spring day in 1994 that, for Russia, was relatively warm – though there was still some snow on the streets – we arrived after a two-hour trip in Kolumna, a city of one hundred forty-eight thousand residents. The city looked miserable; the infrastructure was poorly maintained, and many low buildings seemed on the verge of collapse. Kolumna lies one hundred and twenty kilometers south-east of Moscow, at the confluence of the Moskva and Oka rivers. The city's most important industry today is a diesel locomotive plant.

Until the beginning of the nineties, the famous (and infamous) SS 20 and SS 30 rockets were built in Kolumna. They were mobile ballistic mid-range rockets designed to transport nuclear warheads. Depending on the model, such a rocket could transport a warhead equivalent to seventy-five Hiroshima bombs between six hundred and five thousand kilometers, endangering the strategic equilibrium in Europe. In accordance with the INF (Intermediate Range Nuclear Forces) Treaty, the USSR scrapped the last rocket on May 12, 1991. During the Soviet Era, Kolumna had been a closed city, focused on rocket research and construction. Cyrille Kisselevsky, a Frenchman with Russian roots who, in March, 1996, functioned as the head of the Alfa 2000 Project, asked the inhabitants of Kolumna to explain why, by the end of the Soviet Era, they perceived Kolumna as an open city. See the section entitled, "The organization and financial consolidation phase of Alfa Cement, 1994–1996." The answer: the arrival in the city of monks and nuns who opened two cloisters. People living in closed cities did not experience themselves as prisoners, but rather saw themselves as privileged, since they were paid more and got better goods and food. Also, they could take holidays in specially-reserved hotels located on the Black Sea.

The Director of Shurovsky Tsement, Nikiforov, a friendly man, somewhat plump in stature, met us in front of the factory and immediately invited us to a two-hour inspection of the plant. The leadership style of this man, formerly a director in the red civil service, seemed extremely patriarchal. Nothing had changed since Soviet days. A statue of Lenin still stands at the entrance to the plant, a holy icon of the past, though statues of Stalin have disappeared throughout Russia. In order to reach the chief's office, one must first go to his secretary's office, as everywhere in Russia, a prerequisite for gaining admittance to *the inner sanctum*. The chief's office is typically immense and wood-paneled. Another representation of Lenin, a bust, sits on a ledge behind the comfortable armchair of the Director. After a fairly long conversation, we ask for production and financial figures. The chief's secretary summons the task force responsible for providing these figures – two bookkeepers (in Russia clearly only women hold this position), both with a demeanor that is serious and dignified. They wear identical white blouses with large crocheted collars, a style considered old-fashioned in the West. As we talk, we learn that freight trucks are controlled by the mafia, a factor that leads to increased transport costs. After we enjoy tea and pastries, the mood becomes friendlier and more relaxed. After a while,

Nikiforov slides forward from behind his desk, exposing a carefully camouflaged liquor cabinet; from his stash he offers whisky or vodka as an aperitif to the noonday dinner. As we sip a little glass of vodka, Nikiforov tells us that three or four months ago, when it was still bitterly cold, the police served him with a fine for speeding. As revenge, he turned off the electricity in the Shurovo police office. This was simple to do, he explained, as the power for all of Shurovo comes from the generator in the cement factory. Since then the police have left him alone.

The power and privileges of a factory director, during Soviet times, had little to do with the welfare of the worker and farmer in this much-touted *people's paradise*. Only the managers in the top tiers of the political hierarchy lived on a par with the nobility of the past.

The Soviet art and literature of the twenties – that is, the cultural output produced in the immediate wake of the October Revolution, was characteristically varied and avant-garde. At first the vibrancy of this development was encouraged by the cultural politics of the Bolsheviks, with such progressive visionaries as Kasimir Malevitch and El Lissitzky heading the Moscow Institute of Art. After Stalin seized power in the thirties, however, the avant-garde in art was no longer perceived as useful to the purposes of the state. Propaganda, in the form of *Social Realism*, could better serve the political needs of the new order. Malevitch's works were banned from exhibitions and publications, a casualty of Stalin's repressive dictates in the arts.

We next toured the main building. To my surprise the second floor held an interesting collection of pictures, all well painted in the style of Social Realism. This artistic style, ideological and didactic in purpose, had been approved by the Central Committee of the Communist Party of the Soviet Union in 1932, permeating all avenues of expression – i.e., literature, fine arts, and music. Dedicated wholly to the glory of the industrious farmer and worker, as well as to the brave soldier and his leader, the style flourished most in the period right after the Second World War and continued to enjoy official recognition for many decades thereafter. Yet, by the nineteen eighties and up until the dissolution of the Soviet Union in 1991, an underground in art, neither ideological nor didactic in purpose, was emerging, often exhibited in private lofts and apartments, places that could grant it *unofficial recognition*. In his book, "Memento from Moscow: Meetings with Unofficial Artists, 1978–1997," Paul R. Jolles, the former Swiss diplomat and Secretary of State in the Ministry of Economics, tells of his early visits to now-famous Russian artists who he had cultivated during Soviet times, when their break with official art and their *modernism* seemed all the more powerful and courageous. As one of the first western connoisseurs and collectors of works by this coterie of independent Russian artists, Jolles had taken a particular interest in the work of Illia Kabakov, a conceptual artist, from whom he had bought a number of paintings. For three decades this artist had belonged to the Moscow "Circle of Unofficial Artists." When in 1987, for the first time, Kabakov was allowed to leave the Soviet Union, he expatriated permanently, never to return to Moscow. Today he lives in New York and exhibits his work in all the world's most famous museums.

I returned to Shurovo three times, each time admiring the little collection of pictures on the second floor which had the workings of a cement factory as its theme. One picture in the collection I remember to this day: a horse pulling a sled through a snowy landscape, the sled holding a sack of cement. I was determined to buy one of these pictures from the Shurovo factory. When with delight I showed "my" collection of pictures to Cyrille Kisselevsky, a Frenchman with Russian roots who came from a noble family, and told him of my intention to buy them, he appealed to my conscience and explained that these pictures should remain in the factory as a witness to the past. I did not know then that these figurative pictures, such perfect examples of the style of a particular era, would gain value in the art world for their historical authenticity. As I was to learn much later, some of these Shurovo pictures were taken away by a Holderbank manager who was a connoisseur of art. This occurred after the protagonists of the Russian cement campaign were no longer active in Russia. Without exception, all these pictures were painted in the style of Social Realism, a style whose political and propagandistic imprint had initially blocked my appreciation; only much later could I acknowledge their inherent charm and technical proficiency, even their deserved recognition as monuments to Russia's distinctive history during the Soviet Era.

Painting of a cement kiln in the administrative offices of Shurovo Cement in the style of the Socialist Realism, the officially sanctioned style of art that dominated Soviet painting for 50 years from the early 1930's.

## Chapter 21

## IN THE FAR EAST OF RUSSIA: SPASSK
## NOVEMBER 5–11, 1994

As mentioned previously, Tres Pestalozzi, in Moscow, in May, 1994, had signed the contract with the Alfa Investment Fund, but, for reasons of timing, he was forced to delay his inspection of the Spassk Cement Plant, the largest and, from the Swiss point of view, most important factory in the shares portfolio of the Alfa Investment Fund. The Spassk factory included both a wet and a dry unit.

I was given, along with Dominik, the assignment of preparing for the journey. After briefly organizing this trip, we were able to agree with the others involved on visiting at the end of October, making the necessary bookings and coordinating our trip with Alfa Cement. It was clear from the beginning that Tres was not entirely comfortable with this trip, for it was rumored that the machinations of the mafia were particularly active in the vicinity of Vladivostok and worked seemingly independently because of their great distance from Moscow. It was possible that corruption flourished in high style. Tres had had experience with the mafia in his earlier activity in Italy, but someone in Alfa Cement had explained to him that the Russian mafia differed from the Italian mafia in that one received no previous warning.

In order to calculate with some accuracy the potential risk for a Swiss member of the Executive Committee, I contacted the Swiss Embassy in Moscow and the ABB Ltd. Representative (ABB is a Swiss-Swedish multinational corporation, operating mainly in robots, power, heavy equipment and automation technology) in Vladivostok. Both these sources reassured me that, while one had to be careful, his personal safety was not at risk. Nonetheless, the ABB representative warned me on the telephone that one should never visit the toilet alone in or around Vladivostok. Tres was somewhat reassured by this information and declared that he would come along. Murders in Moscow were constantly being reported in the press and on the radio and television. Early in the morning, just before we left Switzerland, Tres called me at home, saying that he had dreamt he had been kidnapped and had decided that he definitely would not make the trip, but urged us by all means to fly to Spassk as planned.

So we made the thirteen-hour flight from Zürich to Tokyo without Executive Committee Member Pestalozzi. We took a taxi from the Tokyo airport to the main railway station, where three hours later we caught the clean and very punctual Shinkansen, the network running the Japanese high-speed trains to Niigata. To my surprise, Dominik spoke Japanese quite well, for as a twenty-year-old student, he had accompanied the world-famous Polish pianist Krystian Zimerman (born 1956) on a concert tour in Japan. Zimerman was a close friend of Dominik's parents. After waiting two hours, we travelled further toward Niigita, with the bullet-train. This big city, on the major Japanese island Honshu, is three hundred kilometers north of Tokyo. It is the largest port city on the coast of the Sea of Japan. The Niigata railway station is the final station of the Joetsu-Shinkansen, which starts in Ueno. The airport is about eight kilometers northeast of the city center. Niigata is separated from Vladivostok by the Sea of Japan. We wanted to fill in the rather long wait in Niigata by having a good meal in a Japanese restaurant next to the small airport, but unfortunately we did not have any Japanese money, and the restaurant would not take American dollars or our credit cards. In the end, we had to feed on the perfect wax replicas of delicious dishes laid out at the entrance to the restaurant, experiencing the items on the menu only in our imagination, not the real thing. This method of enticing customers into a restaurant is seen throughout Japan, but, in our case, proved to be a cruel enticement – communicating no money, no food. After an Aeroflot flight of over two hours, we finally arrived at the Vladivostok airport. We chose this somewhat roundabout route via Tokyo in order to avoid, at all costs, a long inland flight in Russia. Vladivostok is Russia's most important port city on the Pacific and also the capital of the region (Oblast) Primorje. It is 9,300 kilometers to Moscow by the Trans-Siberian Railway and 6.430 kilometers by air. Incredible as it seems, Vladivostok is seven full time zones away from Moscow! As one of the major ports for the Soviet Pacific Navy, Vladivostok was, until 1991, closed to foreigners. The city is also notable because of its closeness to China (one hundred kilometers to the border) and its connection to Japan by ferry.

To make the following description of our experiences in the far east of Russia more comprehensible, allow me to give a very brief look at history.

Russia reached the Pacific coast for the first time in 1639. More than two centuries later, in the year 1858, the Russian empire annexed the Amur Region of Outer Manchuria, with its somewhat milder climate. Before czarist Russia acquired the sea province through the Treaty of Aigun, the Pacific coast in the Vladivostok region was populated by the Jurchens and the Manchus. This treaty between Russia and the Qing dynasty of China was executed on May 28, 1858, in the Manchurian city of Aigun. It was one of the group of "unequal treaties" which China could be forced to accept in the nineteenth century because of its economic and military weakness. The contract was ratified on June 14, 1858, by the Chinese emperor and on July 20, 1858, by the Russian government, the result of a lengthy Russian expansion into the Amur region and the Far East. The left bank of the Argun River in Amur, down to its mouth at the ocean, was given to Russia, while the right bank, reaching upwards to the Ussuri River, remained the property of China. All told, China lost a part of Manchuria by this treaty, land which had been granted to it in 1689 by the Treaty of Nertschink. Presently, Russia and China share a three-thousand kilometer border.

It was already becoming dark when we walked out of the Vladivostok Airport, where nine people awaited us. Our general director Kharif, with two staff members of Alfa Cement and the head representative from Spassk, were waiting for us with three cross-country vehicles. They were all very disappointed when I explained that Mr. Andrea Pestalozzi had taken ill in Switzerland the evening before our departure and had been told by the doctor that he was not well enough to travel. In contrast to Japan, it was very cold here; the Russians were already wearing winter clothes. We traveled northward, these three jeeps closely following one another. We stopped to get out after about an hour, all three cars stopping at the same place. Only then did I notice that some of the Russians were armed. Clearly Tres had not been entirely wrong in his expectation of danger in this region. While riding in one of the uncomfortable jeeps, I managed to nod off several times, no wonder since we had been travelling twenty eight hours with no real opportunity to grab a good night's sleep. After three hours, the lights of the little city of Spassk-Dalny appeared, a city about one hundred twenty kilometers north of Vladivostok and one hundred kilometers from the Chinese border. It was striking that our companions suddenly relaxed and became talkative. They drove with Dominik and me to an inn and said we should be ready to walk to our supper in forty-five minutes. I had to put the sheets and blankets, found on a chair, on the mattress of the small bed in the little room to which I was shown before I could shower and shave, for the fat and lazy lady at the reception made no effort whatsoever to be helpful. Friendly and welcoming services, so evident in Japan, seemed to have disappeared altogether during the communist regime. Although China and Japan are close by, while Moscow is thousands of kilometers away, it feels here like being in the middle of Russia and not in the Far East. The Caucasian residents without Asiatic features, the style of the houses, the furnishings in the hotels, the food, the saunas, the music, the clothing, and so on are exactly the same as in European Russia. It is astonishing how thick the partition between the once-called *brother states*, China and Russia, must have been. However, globalization and the increasing power of China may end this in the future.

Spassk-Dalny, with about fifty thousand inhabitants, borders on Lake Khanka, which stretches into China. This lake is one hundred kilometers long and eighty kilometers wide; a quarter of the lake belongs to China, the rest to Russia. The city has a station on the Trans-Siberian Railway, which leads from Vladivostok via Khaborovsk to Moscow. The largest enterprise in the city is JSC Spassk Tsement. This cement plant has been in existence since 1907 and has a capacity of 3.5 million tons of cement. In addition to limestone, marble is mined in the vicinity of Spassk-Dalny, and there are large deposits of sand.

After exactly forty-five minutes we are picked up by our hosts, and we walk merrily through the little city, talking higgledy-piggledy, to the canteen for special guests. It was clear that, as the principal employer, the factory heads were also the leaders of this little city and felt safe and at home here. Kharif had fortunately brought along his secretary, Savitzki, who spoke very good English, making it somewhat possible to converse with our hosts, who spoke only Russian. When we entered into the beautifully decorated dining room, we found, as is usual in Russia, mountains of cold delicacies, including good fish from Lake Khanka, and, to drink, beer and vodka, along with flowers on a long and handsomely arranged table. First the Swiss guests were welcomed in Russian, standing and holding a glass of vodka of the usual fifty-gram size. This was followed by drinking speeches and a toast to good health (na zdarovye). After that there were many standing toasts to the health of Russia and Switzerland. Each time a full glass of vodka was swallowed all at once. To be polite I had to do the same. No wonder that still today the average life expectancy of a Russian man is only 61.4 years. For a woman, to be sure, it is 73.9 years.

From 1990 to 1998, the population of Russia remained steadily at one hundred forty-eight million people, but then fell to one hundred forty-two million. The birth rate was stable, but the inadequate medical care caused a high rate of childhood mortality. Also, many Russians had emigrated.

Once the mountain of cold food had been somewhat consumed, there came warm and fatty dishes followed by a nourishing dessert. Weariness was forgotten, the mood was very upbeat. At that time, food throughout Russia was conservative home fare. The Russians knew nothing other than schtschi (cabbage soup), borsch (stew – which included beef, white cabbage, potatoes, carrots, and beets etc. – also called red soup), and plov (rice with meat and carrots). After three hours, we were accompanied back to our modest accommodations. Forty hours had passed since we had left Zürich.

The program the next morning included an inspection of the factory (A/O Spassk Cement). As it was bitterly cold and a strong wind was blowing, and we were not properly dressed, the two Swiss were lent heavy jackets, making us look and almost feel Russian. There were two plants, one wet and the other dry (Spassky and Novospassky), with a total of nine cement ovens and an annual capacity of 3.5 million tons. The cement market in Spassk was bad, as it was throughout Russia. The area was vast, but thinly populated. Here, too, "barter" was the key word – that is to say, sales were generally a matter of exchange of goods. It was difficult, as throughout Russia, to pay the workers in cash. At our last meeting with Kharif, we had already determined whether clinker could be exported to other countries from Vladivostok or to the neighboring harbor, Nakhodka, in order to improve the financial situation of the company.

Automation was not far advanced in the factory. Most of the factories we visited in Russia needed to make a massive investment in dust filters. The cement ovens in Russia were run ninety percent with gas and ten percent with coal. The price of gas at the time was substantially under the international average, so that there was no strong incentive to switch from the wet to the dry system, even though this would require only half the energy. There was practically no capital available, and the cost (interest) for a loan was very high. The factories were run with many workers, so that the labor productivity was three to five times less than in western countries. It also struck us that almost no work was out-sourced: all repairs and maintenance work was done by their own workers, as were the guarding of the plants, the running of social facilities, and the transportation of staff.

We used the afternoon to inspect the social facilities of the two factories, accompanied also by the director of the Sakhalin Factory. These included a large heated swimming pool (in poor condition), a kindergarten, a so-called sanatorium, and a sauna (Banya). In the modest-looking sanitorium, the workers could, among other things, be medically examined. For a small fee, workers could take a mud bath, get a massage, play ping pong, watch television, or read books from the library collection.

When we finally came to the banya reserved for the factory directors, the sauna was already heated and furnished with fresh towels. Drinks (tea and vodka) and pastries stood ready for us on a table. Along with the heads of the factory and a man of diminutive stature – the Russian cement factory manager from Sakhalin, a friend of Kharif, accompanied us on our inspection of the social facilities. In the steam bath, one was to hit each other with birchbranches alternately on the back and the upper leg in order to stimulate the circulation and open the pores. Following this, one cooled off in a cold water pool, situated at the front of the sauna. Our Russian hosts seemed to find this protocol great fun, a symbol of friendship and togetherness. As for cultural offerings of any substance, they were quite modest in this remote place.

On television, in the shabby lobby of our inn, a set with technically miserable transmission, continuously played old black-and-white films with revolutionary themes; for instance, the glorified storming by Bolshevik sailors and workers on November 7, 1917 (Russian – October 24), of the St. Petersburg Winter Palace, then the seat of government. There the Provisional Government had been established under Kerensky, leading to his fall and flight. Lenin demanded the immediate end of the war and the expropriation, without compensation, of large estates, to be given to the farmers and country workers. In January, 1918, the Soviet Union was founded, and Lenin moved the seat of government from St. Petersburg (later known as Leningrad) to Moscow, for strategic military reasons. The last czar and his family were murdered in Yekaterinburg on July 16, 1918. The Bolsheviks wanted to get rid of all the Romanovs in order to avoid a monarchical counter-revolution.

We happened to find ourselves in Spassk on November 7, 1994, precisely on the anniversary of the October Revolution (November 7, 1917).

As described already by Dominik, it seemed to me that communal sauna visits, communal eating and drinking, and caring for the garden of one's dacha after May First (a holiday weekend) were among the few pleasures open to Russians in the Soviet days and still at the time of our visit.

A dacha is a country or holiday house/cottage where city dwellers like to spend their weekends or their summer vacation. The size of the dacha depends solely on the size of the pocket book. Dachas come in all sizes, from huge villas to tiny garden shacks. But most are a simple construction made of wood, a hut or two-story house with a little garden, located in a dacha settlement. As soon as the weather turns warm, all Russian families, every Friday evening, pack swim suits, food, and a thermos, ready to flee to the countryside for a two-day stay. It is customary to plant vegetables and fruit in the garden. Only rarely is there enough space for flowers.

One feels good after two hours in the banya, quite *floppy* and *totally relaxed*. Members of the group invited to this ritual place sweat together through the common experience of the hot sauna, and perhaps also through the drinking that accompanies the bath, so that by the time of coming together again at the large evening meal (comprised of well-known Russian specialties), a feeling of familiarity takes over and personal experiences are exchanged. In this way friendships are established and business connections formed. In order to illustrate the fate of a Volga German, I want to tell the tale of the Sakhalin Factory Manager who was Kharif's friend and who spent a day and an evening with us in Spassk. I will first give a brief explanation.

As Dominik has already mentioned, Volga Germans are descendants of German emigrants who in the years between 1763 and 1767 moved into a new settlement on the Volga at the invitation of the country's Czarina, Katherine II. Katherine the Great (1729–1796) continued her predecessor's politics of opening the country, conquering the Crimea and parts of the Ukraine and Poland. Russia had become an absolute centralized state, following the model of France. The Czarina recruited Germans to cultivate the steppes along the Volga and control the attacks of the horsemen from neighboring districts. By the beginning of the twentieth century, there were already approximately six hundred thousand German settlers in the provinces of Saratov and Samara alone. They were granted a special status, which included the right to maintain German as their language of commerce, the right to self-government, and freedom from military service. As Russian citizens, they populated the greater part of an area comparable to the size of Belgium, about thirty thousand square kilometers.

Stalin seized the Volga Germans' total wheat harvest and sold it abroad. Thousands of Volga Germans died of hunger. On August 28, 1941, after the Nazi-German occupation of the Soviet Union, the Supreme Soviet of the USSR issued the following decree, "The entire German population living in the Volga Region, now numbering only about four hundred thousand, are declared guilty of collaboration with the enemy, to be resettled in Siberia and Kazakhstan." As a result of this edict, more than thirty percent of these resettled Germans died in labor camps and gulags.

At supper, after the sauna, the manager of the Sakhalin Factory told us that his mother was Russian, his father German – from whom he had learned only broken German. This son of mixed parentage had fled a labor camp in Kazakhstan and had walked thousands of kilometers eastward, mostly at night. He survived on berries and roots and occasionally on fish. When he finally reached the Pacific, he was able to take a fishing boat to the island of Sakhalin, where he hid. At the end of his tragic but admirable tale, told almost in a monotone, he pulled up his sleeve and showed us his arm, still bearing the tattooed number from the gulag. I was full of admiration for his enormous determination and his ability to survive. I was amazed that he had no unkind words for the regime that had treated him and his family in such a cruel and inhumane fashion.

We never heard in the stories of other Russians a wish for revenge or tirades expressed against the cruelty and oppression inflicted on them by the communist regime. The Russians seemed to us to have an unlimited capacity for suffering.

The gulag has become a synonym for the comprehensive system of repression in the Soviet Union, consisting of forced labor camps, concentration camps, prison camps, and areas of exile. They supported the suppression of political opponents, exploitation through forced labor, and the internment of prisoners of war. The system of camps was an essential element of Stalin's rule.

Even the Russian czars had exiled political prisoners to Siberia (Katorga), but that involved many fewer people than were exiled to camps under the Soviets, a number that at times reached two and one-half million prisoners. It is estimated that a total of eighteen million people suffered in these camps during the communist reign of terror, which lasted seventy years. The inhumane living conditions led to the death of hundreds of thousands of prisoners. The first critical literature about the gulags appeared in the Soviet Union during the thaw. The most outstanding work from this time is probably Aleksander Solzhenitsyn's, "A Day in the Life of Ivan Denisovich." Solzhenitsyn's work, "The Gulag Archipelago," appeared in foreign countries in the nineteen seventies and had the effect of making the word "gulag" understood universally as *a political system of repression exercised uniquely in the Soviet Union.*

The next day we visited the main building of Spassk. Alfa Cement had already begun to buy shares in Spassk. Kharif decided to delegate Anatoly from Alfa Cement to spend six weeks in Spassk,

At the quarry of Spassk Tsement in November 1994.
From right: D. Wlodarczak, works director, author.

to purchase on the spot a greater number of shares until finally reaching the majority. A due diligence examination was impossible. As evening fell, we drove from the factory to the inn in Spassk-Dalny. In an open field we saw a drunk lying in a ditch in the snow, in icy cold weather. We stopped and took him with us, as he would have otherwise soon frozen to death.

## Chapter 22

TRAVELING FURTHER FROM SPASSK TO NAKHODKA
AND THEN TO VLADIVOSTOK
NOVEMBER 1994

Early the next morning we again headed south, in two large Toyota four-wheel drive vehicles; but we did not go back to Vladivostok, going instead towards Nakhodka. The route took us for some time on a slightly hilly road along the Pacific coast. The loud-speakers in the two cars played Russian hits almost without a break; by the end of the long trip, we practically knew these popular songs by heart. Suddenly, in the sea, we saw partially rusted war ships laying crookedly on their sides, only half submerged in the water. Only then did we notice that we were driving past the Russian port for atomic submarines. The now bygone Soviet Union had built, in its heyday, a total of two hundred and forty four atomic submarines. Since then, more than one hundred and eighty had been withdrawn from service. At the beginning of the nineties, Russia had a very limited capacity to break up these submarines and to dispose of them in an ecologically sound manner. We could now see this clearly, giving us an uneasy feeling that the area might be polluted with atomic waste. The housing for the sailors seemed quite modest. We were surprised when a young Russian woman appeared at the side of the road, her hair well groomed, sporting a long, elegant leather coat; shortly after taking note of her, we saw her disappear into one of the rundown barracks. The Russians had brought an ample lunch, a meal we consumed while standing in the sand, close by the tailgates of the two vehicles. All around us was the powerful wind and roaring Pacific, though unlike other Pacific regions, the sky and sea in this area is grey, not the expected blue. Yet, despite these few drawbacks, the world, once again, resumed a sense of order.

Having one hundred sixty-five thousand inhabitants, Nakhodka is among the cities furthest east in Russia. It is on the Bay of Nakhodka, on the Sea of Japan, a good nine thousand kilometers southeast of Moscow and eighty-five kilometers east of Vladivostok. Its importance lies in the fact that it is the commercial transfer point between ships in the Sea of Japan and the Russian railway system. As in Vladivostok, it has the monsoon climate typical of far eastern Russia, with cold dry winters and windy, damp summers that frequently turn into raging typhoons. Until the end of the Soviet Union, Nakhodka was highly significant for western tourists as the final terminal of the Trans-Siberian Railway and the ferry harbor for Japan, functions not available in Vladivostok; as the seat of the Soviet Pacific Fleet, Vladivostok was closed to foreigners.

When we finally arrived in Nakhodka, we immediately noticed a large coal terminal on the harbor; from this coal terminal, we learned, Siberian coal was shipped to Japan. We inspected the infrastructure of the harbor with a view to finding a suitable place for exporting clinker from Spassk and discussed this with the local authorities. We spent the night in a modest Chinese hotel and learned that houses were frequently unheated and sometimes had no warm water and that electricity was available only a few hours each day. We noted once again the small, simple wooden Russian houses with elaborate woodcut trimmings, looking just like those around Moscow. They reminded me of Marc Chagall's romantic pictures of Russia. I found it astonishing that this type of wooden construction was to be found in the far eastern part of Russia, in very sparsely populated areas very close to over-populated China, which had a completely different style of building and a far more dynamic economy. In the whole of Siberia, which comprises about three-quarters of the territory of Russia, there are only about twenty-five million inhabitants; the average population per square kilometer is 2.7 people. And it is evident that someday China with its economic and military power could try to correct the "inequality" (as described above) and call into question the Russian presence in parts of Siberia and the region around Vladivostok.

The next day, when we left Nakhodka and came to Vladivostok, we visited the harbor authorities, who impressed all of us as not serious and as mostly interested in money. Later, as we walked along the harbor, Savitzki reminded us once again that this city had been closed to foreigners until over two years ago and that a Swiss colonel such as the author would have been arrested immediately and would have mysteriously disappeared for a long time. As twilight drew on, our official mission was ended, and we said goodbye to Kharif and his associates. We were taken to a modern-looking Japanese hotel, hoping secretly that this time the heat, the water, and the electricity would work. The rooms we were shown on the seventh floor looked modern, and it seemed as though everything would work. I was already looking forward to a warm shower and a well-earned supper. No sooner had I taken off my shirt with the object of enjoying the warm shower that everything went completely dark in the room. I contacted Dominik in a neighboring room. After a long search he had found a flashlight and waited outside the door for me until I was completely dressed again. As the lift was also not working, we made our way carefully down the narrow winding stairs, one floor at a time, Dominik going ahead of me with a flashlight that provided only a dim beam. Fortunately, we found a candle-lit bar on the ground floor, by the entrance to the hotel. There were no lights on the tables, so we sat with a few other hotel guests at the bar and got drinks and even a little cold supper. After an hour, the electricity began to work again, and we noticed only then that an attractive young blond had sat down next to us. As we could not speak a word of Russian, she soon tired of us, probably assessing us as two inarticulate Swiss clods. But we noticed in our Russian travels that Russian women were distinctly emancipated and flaunted their sexuality. On the other hand, the men tried to order their women around and displayed their machismo, as the following anecdote illustrates.

After a session in Moscow with the management of Alfa Cement I went out for a beer with some of those present. There was an impassioned discussion of the sex scandal concerning President Clinton and his intern, Monica Lewinsky. The Russians found it mystifying that the world press paid so much attention to such a situation, that the president of the United States almost lost his job because of it, and that so much of the American population was so obsessed with this matter. The Russians were of the opinion that no one here in Russia would get excited about such a bagatelle; on the contrary, they would be glad to have such a good-looking and virile president. There are enough willing women here, and surely no one would speak of a scandal.

The next day we found ourselves once again in a plane from Vladivostok to Tokyo, and everything functioned extremely well from the first. The information service in the airport, the hotel staff where we spent the night, and the saleswomen were in comparison to Russia as day is to night. Russia still embraced the culture of the Soviet Union, ruled by a supreme government and having a corresponding unfriendly service mentality.

In the already mentioned book, "Russen sind Anders" ["Russians are Different"], Gisela Tobler and Karl Eckstein describe the approach to service in the Soviet Union. "Restaurants were closed at noon, the thinking being that the personnel are eating their lunch and therefore cannot be serving guests. The stores were specifically open when people were at work, or at least should be. Nobody thought of having convenient open hours. Everyone let the state serve them, but no one wanted to work …Ordinary citizens had to wait for hours in snow storms and endless rain for a bus, while party bosses drove by in grand limousines and bought the best vodka in bottles with stoppers in their stores. In contrast, the vodka bottles of pedestrians were closed with a flap that usually ripped when it was opened so that one had to fiddle around with a needle and a knife before reaching the contents."

When we took the Swissair plane from Tokyo to Zürich, I was seated next to the well-known Swiss ambassador and business diplomat Arthur Dunkel, from 1980 to 1993 Director-General of the General Agreement on Tariffs and Trade (GATT) in Geneva. I had met him previously, but briefly. He was very active in the Uruguay Round of Multilateral Trade Negotiations, and when the negotiations stalled, he drafted the famous "Dunkel Draft." This proposal was adopted with few changes by all participating countries and subsequently became the foundation of the World Trade Organization (WTO). We had a pleasant conversation, and he told me, among other things, that he had come to Japan because he supported young Japanese artists.

After we returned to Switzerland, Alfa-Bank purchased more shares in Spassk. Anatoli from Alfa-Cement was delegated to Spassk for six weeks in order to buy vouchers for shares on the spot until a majority of shares was attained. This goal was in fact achieved.

Lunch at the windy pacific beach between Nakhodka and Vladivostok.

## Chapter 23

ENTER THE WORLD BANK (IFC)
NEGOTIATIONS FROM AUTUMN 1994 TO WINTER 1995–96

After we had signed the contract and the Holderbank portfolio of shares in Alfa-Cement was official, the World Bank heard about it. We were subsequently contacted by Khosrov Zamani, the regional leader for Eastern Europe at the International Finance Corporation (IFC), a branch of the World Bank. When he first telephoned us, he wanted to know if Holderbank would be interested in IFC financing for Alfa Cement, which would lead to greater growth of the group and strengthening of its position in the market. We had a positive view of bringing in the IFC, as having such an important partner would make us less vulnerable, despite Kharif's good network, and would make it easier to protect our interests were we for any reason to experience political pressure or legal difficulties. At the same time, additional financial resources would let Alfa Cement purchase additional shares, set up marketing approaches (especially in Moscow), and undertake certain types of investment in the plants. Using the IFC's right to stock options, Holderbank could win time in that it could build up its supply of shares if, in a couple of years, IFC pulled out and the risks in Russia had become clearer. All these reasons spoke in favor of engaging the IFC. We had an initial meeting with Zamani in Moscow, after which our Russian partner agreed to bring in the IFC.

Zamani wanted to arrange an eventual investment of Alfa Cement in cooperation with ING Barings Bank. IFC had evidently completed a number of transactions in Russia with Barings and wanted to be included in a part of Barings' structuring. The head of Barings in Moscow was the American Richard Sobel, who had worked for several years at the European Bank for Reconstruction and Development (EBRD) and who spoke good Russian. This man, who had a Harvard MBA, impressed me at that time with his calmly stated but precise arguments. Today he is the CEO of Alfa Capital Partners, a private equity firm founded in 2003 specializing in management buyouts.

There followed a number of negotiation sessions in which the participation of IFC/Barings as a third party was established. IFC/Barings executed a due diligence before this could be written into a declaration of intent. As part of this examination, we toured the factories in Shurovo, Gornosavodsk, and Volsk with Zamani and one of his analysts. On the basis of the data from the due diligence and the factory visits, IFC proposed to join Alfa Cement with twenty million US dollars. This defined, at the same time, clear areas of investment for using the capital contributed by IFC/Barings. IFC also stipulated that Alfa Cement had to sign a management contract with Holderbank, obliging Holderbank to furnish concrete support to the restructuring and increased productivity of Alfa Cement. The negotiations concerning the contract continued into the winter of 1995–96. Chadbourne & Park was again involved on our side, while IFC/Barings received legal counsel from Norton Rose Fulbright, a global law firm with 58 offices around the world. The entrance of IFC/Barings was ratified in the spring of 1996.

In 2007 I ran into Khosrov Zamani in Almaty, Kazakhstan, where he held a leadership position in the European Bank (EBRD), and we spoke almost nostalgically about the exciting days in Moscow, 1994–96. I was in Almaty at that time on a mission in my capacity as Swiss Honorary Counsel to the Republic of Kazakhstan. This immense country of steppes – as big as the whole of Western Europe – holds enormous amounts of oil and of underground treasures. Since its declaration of independence in 1991, the president, Nursultan Nasarbayev, rules unopposed and autocratically a population of only fifteen million people with a mixture of pragmatism and visionary ideas. Before the fall of the Soviet

Union he was already, as General Secretary of the Communist Party of the Kazakh Socialist Soviet Republic, the most powerful man in the country. I found it interesting to observe how his government is making a successful attempt to forge an identity for this huge but sparsely settled region. The Russians, still half of the population at the time of independence, are now only about one third of the population, while two-thirds of the people are Asiatic. In the ministries and also in the shops almost only Russian is spoken in daily life, but the Asiatic majority population often speak another language at home, a Turkic language. The children of the one-time Russians must also now learn to speak the Turkic language in kindergarten. The new nationalism helps the people of the country, once a Soviet republic, to coalesce and to forge a new identity of their own.

Let me add that in 2002 I received a call from Markus Oberle (from Holcim), then the CEO of Alfa Cement in Moscow, asking if, as the Honorary Counsel to Kazakhstan, I could help him to arrange to export sulphur-resistant cement from the Volsk factory on the Volga to Kazakhstan, as this special type of cement was needed in the oil fields on the Caspian Sea and was not produced by any of the Kazakh cement factories. With the assistance of the Kazakh ambassador in Bern, I was subsequently able to arrange a meeting in Geneva with the Industry and Commerce Minister of the Republic of Kazakhstan. A mere two months later use of the Russian special cement was approved by the Kazakh authorities and the sale of this imported cement from Russia was able to begin.

## Chapter 24

## BY PRIVATE PLANE FROM MOSCOW TO PERM
## SEPTEMBER 1995

Because of the infusion of capital from Holderbank, and later from IFC/Barings, Alfa Cement, under the leadership of Kharif, was able to acquire, within a short period of time, shares in various important companies, most particularly in Shurovo and Spassk and, in effect, to control these companies. Alfa Cement was now the largest cement group in Russia. But the centralized management of all the companies under its aegis (i.e., Gornosavodsk, Volsk, Spassk, and Shurovo) was still inadequate; it was high time to create an efficient central organization that would bring synergy to the companies controlled by Alfa Cement as well as consider options for other companies in the group; should shares in these other (less strategic) companies continue to be retained and enhanced or should they be sold. Of these, only Novoros on the Black Sea had strategically important minority holdings.

It was definitely necessary to determine exactly what was going on in Perm in the Urals, as the main office of Alfa Cement was located there and, as such, always employed more staff. Tres Pestalozzi, who was very busy with other acquisitions in Eastern Europe, always attended the Board Meetings of Alfa Cement, but often could not join the time-consuming trips to the individual plants in Russia. (In the meantime, I, also, had become a member of the Alfa Cement board of Directors.)

In order to ease the stress of arranging air transportation for our business trips within Russia, Dominik and I turned to Kharif for some practical advice. From this discussion, we learned that chartering a Russian jet was not much more expensive than purchasing individual passenger tickets on a regular commercial flight. Most importantly, the customized treatment afforded by a chartered jet company enabled us to avoid the usual long waits one encounters at airports designed for large-scale passenger air transport. As almost no one at Holderbank was interested in Russia, and because we proceeded discreetly in arranging our trips there, the danger of our actions provoking a tidal wave of ugly rumors generated by envious colleagues was minimal. Tres, like us, saw the budgetary outlay required for chartering flights within Russia to be quite modest, especially as viewed in the context of how they so greatly satisfied our air travel needs. Kharif had arranged for Nikiforov, his long-time confidant from Moscow and, presently, the manager of the plant in Shurovo, to fly with us; also to accompany us was Savitzki, a court translator who lived in Moscow. Nikiforov, a man of strong personality traits, had integrated without difficulty into the Alfa Cement Group. These men, comprising *the entire Russian delegation*, were punctually waiting for us at the Moscow Airport. The crew of the chartered Aeroflot plane treated us royally, the food offered us representing an important part of this *royal treatment*. The seating was ample, even spacious, affording each of us more than enough room to assure our comfort. After just a short period of time, the Russian champagne flowed and worked its magic, putting us into a festive mood and, in the case of the Russians, loosening some tongues. From this wonderfully relaxed mood, came the narratives of a few scandalous incidents. The one I remember most came from Savitzki:

A poor babushka (is a grandmother with a head scarf), stationed in front of the Kremlin Wall, sold beets that came from Chernobyl (on August 26, 1986, there had been a catastrophic reactor accident in the atomic plant at Chernobyl) at a price much higher than that charged by the other beet sellers. An interested seller inquired into these high-priced beets and asked the babushka what was so special about the beets from Chernobyl. The answer: my beets are particularly suitable for wicked stepmothers!

In Perm at the headquarter we were greeted in Kharif's almost elegant and well-appointed offices, facilities he had adeptly arranged for early in his assignment to this town. He introduced us to his staff of mostly new and young co-workers. The only ones I remember are Stanislav Arkhipov, Alex Kruppa, and Olga Kochova. Kharif's pretty daughter had also received an appointment on his staff. Dominik and I had the uneasy feeling that Kharif had taken on an over-sized staff, perhaps due to an inflated notion of his position – with dreams of building his own little empire. Following the introductions to members of his staff, we were presented with a well-prepared report of the share participations of the respective companies in the group and the steps to be taken next. The cashflow and overall budget of the group was quite modest, we were told, because of the still-depressed cement prices, facts that spoke to the need for exercising measures of thrift. Among other things, we talked about the fact that the extensive *social* arrangements at the various factories in the group (indoor swimming pools, saunas, sanatoria, kindergartens, sports grounds, etc.) were no longer feasible given the still-sinking Russian economy; the expensive social arrangements had to be transferred to the respective communities. To discuss these problems at greater length, we spent the evening with a total of twelve gentlemen at an elegant, undoubtedly expensive, restaurant in Perm.

It became clear to us that we needed to appoint to the central office a Holderbank staff member, someone who was competent and dependable and who spoke fluent Russian. I suggested to Tres that we employ Cyrille Kisselevsky, a man who had worked earlier as the head of human resources at Ciments d'Origny, Holderbank's branch in France. I did not know at that time that Cyrille's father, who had fled to France in 1922, belonged to the old nobility or that his grandfather had commanded a regiment under the czar.

Under the rule of Katherine the Great, the Russian nobility (dvoryanstvo) received, in 1785, total rights to rule the peasants under them. This law was changed under Czar Alexander II through the 1886 law ending the right of bondage. The 1917 October Revolution put an end to the nobility. Many nobles were persecuted, imprisoned, or shot. Cyrille's father fled to Paris in 1922 and later sent Cyrille, who was born in Paris, to the Russian school in Paris, which he attended once a week, on Saturdays. Only after 1991 were organizations of the nobility and their traditions once again permitted in Russia. In July, 1998, the mortal remains of the czar's family were transported from Yekaterinburg to St. Petersburg and given a ceremonial interment in the Peter and Paul Cathedral in the presence of President Yeltsin. Today the Russian population is interested in their pre-Revolutionary past and also in the families of the former nobility.

Cyrille Kisselevsky had lived with his wife in a tiny apartment near the Hotel Ukraine since 1996. He told us that this was a luxurious apartment compared to the small communal apartments (kommunalkas) in which most other people were housed. Shortly after the seizure of power in October 1917, the Bolsheviks in Moscow began the takeover of large apartment buildings, particularly those belonging to upper-class bourgeoisie and aristocrats, at the same time dividing up the expropriated apartments for the proletariat. Khrushchev supported the development of social housing. New quarters were built at the edge of the city with standard and ready-made materials. These became known as "Khrushchevchoby", a distortion of the word "truschtschoby," meaning a wretched neighborhood. In the so-called *workers' paradise* of the Soviet Union, the majority of the urban workers lived in miserable communal apartments, in old deteriorating buildings. A whole family lived in each room of the unit, while they all had to share the kitchen and toilet, a true horror by western standards. This led to constant friction among the various families sharing a unit. Until the middle of the nineteen nineties, most Moscow residents still lived in such communal apartments. When, later in the nineties, the housing market was privatized, many hopeful Muscovites, for little money, were able to purchase housing in cheaply-constructed apartment buildings, located at the edge of the city. These new apartments offered families who had been living in incredibly small communal quarters the chance to live quite cheaply in their own apartment. To have their own apartment, however modest or inconveniently located, was, for these people, the realization of a long-held dream. In the process of implementing this relocation plan, the so-called s*mart alecs* surfaced, people slick enough to effectuate the vacancy of choice real estate, large centrally-located units, for their own purposes. These they would renovate either for their own use or for sale at a high price. Kisselevsky figured that by now only about ten percent of Moscow residents still lived in communal apartments.

According to Cyrille, the old Soviet heating system was tricky. Almost every building in the big cities was attached to a remote district heating system and could not be regulated within apartments. The district heating was not turned on until the average temperature was less than eight degrees Celsius (46 F) for five

The spacious interior of the rented private plane in September 1995. Left: D. Wlodarczak and besides the author.

days running. Since in most apartments the heat could not be regulated and there were no vents, let alone thermostats, opening the window was often the only way to stop one's living room from becoming a sauna when the winter brought Siberian sub-zero temperatures. So most apartments were either too hot or too cold, especially when the heat furnished in May was the same as that furnished during the coldest days of winter.

The next day we met with the VIP service at two in the afternoon, at the Perm Airport and were taken directly to our private plane, which was ready to take off for our return trip to Moscow. Our notes show that we were again spoiled and treasured the luxury of a private plane.

# Chapter 25

MOSCOW-KOLUMNA, MOSCOW-PERM
MARCH 20–23, 1996

Almost no one in leadership positions at Holderbank, except Andreas Pestalozzi and Anton E. Schrafl, took an interest in working in Russia, either at the beginning of ironing out a partnership with the Russians or thereafter. As described above, Toni had been interested in speaking with the Russian delegation at the WEF meeting in Davos in February, 1996, and had invited me to join them. Ever since I have known him, Toni has been a true visionary among the top echelon at Holderbank. His predictions about coming trends in the cement industry and about the economic and political developments likely to emerge in western and eastern countries have, as a rule, been correct, although sometimes not until many years later. During his studies at the Swiss Federal Institute of Technology in Zürich, he took Russian language lessons, back during the Cold War days when Russia was despised. My proposal that he join us on a trip to inspect cement works in Russia pleased him so greatly that he decided to bring along his charming wife Catherine. Dominik and I were not entirely selfless in issuing this invitation, for it gave us a chance to have, on-the-spot, the intellectual input of an opinion leader who believed in the potential of Russia. This connection to such an articulate and accomplished man boosted our secretly nourished hope of developing a portfolio of promising acquisitions in the Russian cement industry, a hope that, in this early stage of connecting to Russia, seemed quite capable of attainment. If all went well at this initial stage, further advantageous acquisitions in the Russian cement industry would follow.

Before the projected trip could take place, Toni informed me, in his Zürich office, that he would come only if I could get him a small Geiger counter. I started at once to look for such an item in Zürich and soon found a Geiger counter in the form of a watch that could be worn on one's wrist. I bought such a special watch for Tres as well. I surmised that Toni suspected there was still radiation in the Urals because of the concentration there of many atomic factories whose focus on atomic testing might have produced consequences akin to the fallout that had resulted in the aftermath of the Chernobyl accident.

We all flew all together by Swissair to Moscow, where we stayed at the tried-and-true Hotel Metropol, a first-class accommodation where I was able to negotiate a favorable corporate rate. The next day we took a chartered plane to Perm. We were picked up graciously by Kharif and the management of Gornosavodsk and taken at once to a small nameless luxury hotel with a strong fence around it, located at the edge of the city and completely hidden from the world at large. Until three years ago it was reserved solely for highly placed party bigwigs (members of the nomenclatura). As Tres wanted to hold talks immediately with Kharif and his associates, we arranged for Toni to go by helicopter directly to the Gornosavodsk Cement Factory. Toni was delighted with this flight over the wide-spread forests, all the more because the Geiger counter never really registered. Tres, on the other hand, had more *luck* on a separate helicopter flight, from Gornosavodsk to Perm. As he explained, the Geiger counter began to tick intensely as they flew over certain buildings, as strongly as one would encounter in a passenger plane at an altitude of ten kilometers. As if this wasn't enough to shake the confidence of any passenger on this flight, a bucket, dangling in the middle of the helicopter, under the gears, served, as he learned, to conserve the overflowing oil needed in preparation for the next flight. And the rusty nail that secured a huge trapdoor in the floor of the helicopter was just about the last straw for Tres, destroying any confidence he tried so desperately to maintain despite the telltale signs of a risky flight.

We all flew comfortably back to Moscow in the same chartered plane. Kharif had already arranged for a visit of Tres and the vice-chairman of the Holderbank Financiere Board of Directors to meet with the top leadership of Alfa-Bank. We arrived at this meeting a few minutes early and therefore waited in front of the bank for the expected arrival of Mikhail Fridman and Piotr Aven, who appeared punctually a few minutes later. A large armored Mercedes and two accompanying vehicles arrived at the main entrance of Alfa-Bank. Bodyguards from the accompanying vehicles immediately surrounded the Mercedes, checking in every direction before opening the door. The two top executives of Alfa-Bank then finally emerged. In contrast to Aven, Fridman was rather stocky; he had a round face and, generally, a brawny appearance. He looked the way every little Swiss boy thinks a slippery Russian businessman should look. The numbers one and two, that is, the two most important shareholders in the bank, greeted us warmly and invited us into a conference room.

Mikhail Fridman's business career followed a phenomenal course. He was born into a Jewish family from Lemberg. As a student at the Moscow Institute for Steel and Metallurgy, he took on various jobs that, at the time, under the Soviet regime, were illegal, such as washing windows and running a discotheque (as private enterprises), but also establishing a sort of theater ticket booth, mafia-style. In the more liberal days under Gorbachev, when he was an employee in a company for construction building, Fridman founded cooperatives for various types of businesses, for instance, a real estate office that serviced foreigners, a cigarette and perfume import business, a computer firm, and so forth. Two years after he finished his studies, he founded the "Alfa Eco Group," which was connected with the Swiss enterprise, "ADP Trading," and imported sugar, tea, cigarettes, and other goods to Russia. In 1992 Alfa received a license for exporting Russian petroleum. The Alfa Group grew out of these beginnings. Fridman's partner was Piotr Aven. According to

Forbes, Fridman's assets reached twenty billion US dollars three years ago, while Aven's wealth was also estimated to be in billions of US dollars.

We held an intense and extremely interesting conversation with the two oligarchs, during which we determined that they were very well informed about the details concerning Holderbank and its work in Russia. Good connections with two of the most powerful oligarchs in Russia could only be advantageous.

Early the next day, in several vehicles, we left for Kolumna, a factory situated near the Shurovo Cement Factory. We inspected the plant and the quarry and, in a conference room, had an interesting conversation with the director of the plant, Nikiforov. Kharif and his most important co-worker, as well as Kisselevsky, were also present.

In front of the headquarters of Alfa-Bank March 1996:
M.Fridmann welcomes a representative of Alfa Cement. From right: A. Pestalozzi, A. Schrafl (from behind)

Meeting with the director of the plant in Shurovo. The first to right ist Anton Schrafe, opposite his wife.

P. Aven (left) and M.Fridman

## Chapter 26

## ORGANIZATIONAL AND FINANCIAL CONSOLIDATION PHASE OF ALFA CEMENT
## 1994–96

Once we had signed the contract concerning shares (May, 1994), we began to work out a specific plan of action for increasing efficiency. Dominik proposed such a plan, including goals and means (Alfa-2000-Project). We needed more qualified staff on the Alfa team to carry out this plan. Our highest priority was to bring about transparency and clarity in the financial development of the individual Alfa cement groups involved in the acquisition of shares. For this we hired Andrei Malyutin, a young Russian controller who spoke good English and was familiar with international accountancy standards. His task was to introduce a clear reporting system which could reasonably be used to run Alfa Cement. It was not easy to find someone with the necessary qualifications who also had the flexibility needed to work for some time in widely dispersed cement factories and to live under the hard conditions imposed by those locations. We found the right person in Malyutin.

Holderbank appointed Ray Cunningham to serve as director of the Volsk factory. This tried-and-true, imperturbable "cement legionnaire" packed up his things and moved with his wife and child to the deepest province on the Volga and performed peerless pioneer work. Using a satellite station, he created his own access to the internet, the telephone, and western television. With these aids, his wife was able to home-school their daughter and enrich her lessons via access to appropriate educational material. This self-sufficient family planted vegetables, thus providing some of their own food.

Holderbank also supported the education and further development of Alfa Cement's workers by inviting them to internal courses and conferences in Switzerland and other countries. A worker was to complete a half-year practicum at a Holderbank plant in the USA. After all this was discussed and organized, the departure of the Alfa Cement employee was delayed for unexplained reasons. He then inexplicably disappeared from Russia and suddenly appeared at Holderbank in the USA. It turned out that he had purposely delayed his departure so that his pregnant wife could give birth during their stay in America, making their child automatically an American citizen.

## Chapter 27

## ARTISTIC EXPERIENCES DURING OUR TIME IN RUSSIA
## 1993–1998

When the first months after the signing of the contract had passed and we had increasingly to address the rationalization of the group, we had more time in Moscow to turn to cultural interests between sessions. Like many tourists, we visited the Kremlin, which, with its impressive orthodox cathedrals and gilded interiors, made a lasting impression on me. The interiors of the churches in particular radiated something both ceremonial and sacred, with their many icons. According to legend, Stalin would not let the cathedrals in the Kremlin be touched, out of a fear of God. In a report issued in a 1948 edition of Der Spiegel, a French journalist wrote, with the approval of official Soviet authorities, that religion was a superstitious holdover from the capitalist past which would disappear once the Russian people were reeducated into the materialistic spirit of Marx and Engels. The constitution gave neither clergy nor their family the right to vote, and the children of the clergy could not attend universities. By 1921, about fifteen hundred cloisters, centuries-old, were partially destroyed. Under Stalin about two hundred thousand orthodox clergy had been arrested by 1940, and one hundred thousand of them were murdered. In his investigation into religion in Russia, the French journalist determined that while the majority of the churches in the Soviet capital had been destroyed or were being used for secular purposes, forty of them were available for religious services. In 1931, Stalin had the Cathedral of Christ the Redeemer blown up in order to have the "Palace of the Soviet People" erected in its place, which at a height of four hundred and fifteen meters was the tallest building in the world, a symbol of the unlimited power of the Soviet Union. But the palace remained a castle in the air, and in 1960 a swimming pool was built in the foundations of the church. Just forty years later, the Moscovites rebuilt the Cathedral of Christ the Redeemer according to its original plan, for about one hundred seventy million US dollars (Neue Zürcher Zeitung, Nov. 11, 2011).

The Kremlin is a fortress with thick walls and twenty towers that was constructed in its present form between 1485 and 1499 and remains in good condition. The dark red brick wall of the citadel measures a total of 2,235 meters in length (2,444 yards). Ever since 1990, the Kremlin and Red Square have been cited on the UNESCO list of world treasures.

In March, 2001, I had an opportunity to revisit the Kremlin as a participant in a mission that included representatives and economists of the Swiss government under the leadership of Federal Counselor/Minister Pascale Couchepin. This time I was able to view the impressive Hall of Armaments, an exhibition space which, along with armaments, houses such historical symbols of power as jewels (including diamonds), coronation insignia, historical weapons, costly garments, state coaches, carriages, and sleds – an outstanding array of precious items, set forth to be admired. Most impressive were the Faberge eggs, the epitome of masterful craftsmanship. Between 1885 and 1916, the jeweler Peter-Carl Faberge created fifty eggs for the czar's family. These egg-shaped pieces, given by the czar to his family as an annual tradition in celebration of orthodox Easter, are decorated with precious stones (including pearls) set in filigree, alongside of gold, and ivory carvings. Today considered the essence of luxury, each individual piece contains a hidden jewel within, conveying a personal connection to the czar's family. In February, 2004, the Russian oligarch Viktor Vekselberg purchased ten eggs for about one hundred million US dollars, funds raised through his "Link of Times Cultural and Historical Foundation."

We delighted in viewing the Tretyakov Gallery, a sort of national shrine. This art collection of five thousand eight hundred pictures was put together by Pavel Tretyakov (1832–1898) with his inherited money and the money he made from the textile industry.

I was particularly pleased by the collection of old Russian artifacts, an exhibit first opened in Soviet times, when the most important Russian icons were taken from churches and placed in the museum. Many Russian orthodox cathedrals and cloisters were blown up, torn down, or put to other uses by Stalin. The persecution of the churches in the Soviet Union began in 1917, immediately after the October Revolution. All religious instruction and publications were banned.

The Pushkin Museum was another impressive experience. It was only after the October Revolution that the museum became famous, after private collections were seized and given to the museum. Noteworthy are the collections of the patrons Ivan Morosov and Sergei Schtschukin, which contained outstanding works of classical modernism and which were divided equally between the Hermitage in St. Petersburg and the Pushkin Museum. Paintings from the Tretyakov Collection expanded the collection of French paintings, which belong among the most important outside France. We never would have thought such a fine collection of European art would be preserved in Moscow after such a long period of communist domination and the style of Social Realism propagated by the regime had prevailed, a style which gave heroic stature to the literal construction of the Soviet Union by the ordinary citizenry (hero farmers, workers and military). As mentioned already, a multiplicity of first-rate avant-garde art (for instance, by Kasimir Malevich, the founder of Constructivism) and literature developed, surprisingly, in the Soviet Union right after the October Revolution, particularly in the twenties and the early thirties, in contrast to the state-approved art that developed later initiated by Stalin.

Somehow bizarre are the over-sized iron statues by the Georgian artist Surab Zereteli, dispersed here and there throughout Moscow.

They were commissioned by the very powerful and long-serving mayor of Moscow, Yuri Luzhkov. He erected a ninety-four meter high (103 yards) memorial for Peter the First on a manmade island between the Moscow River and the by-pass canal. This memorial for Peter the Great was originally supposed to depict Christopher Columbus, but because neither the Dominican Republic nor Venezuela nor Brazil wanted to have a memorial celebrating the five hundredth anniversary of the discovery of America by Zereteli. Luzhkov as a friend of Zereteli came to the rescue.

Quite close to the small but typical apartment of Cyrille Kisselevsky stood the Hotel Ukraine, completely renovated since 2010 and now called the Radisson Royal Hotel Moscow. The two hundred and eight meter (207 yards) tall skyscraper, with its towers, columns, and Soviet stars, is one of the so-called "Seven Sisters," commissioned by Stalin in Moscow after the Second World War in the typical pompous and lofty *gingerbread style.* These included the foreign ministry, the Lomonosov University, and the Leningrad Hotel.

At first I found these buildings repulsive, as I had not encountered this style anywhere else in the world. To my surprise, I became used to it and would actually regret it if they were torn down. These buildings, at least, remind us of the one-time capital of the world revolution. Unfortunately, there are only a few buildings left from that time. On the positive side, it can be noted that in the last few years a good deal of money has been contributed to the preservation of historical structures. Today Moscow has become not only the political, but also the economic capital. A number of chrome-and-glass towers along the Moscow River now employ well over one hundred thousand workers and represent the highest tower in Europe (Rossiya), which stretches six hundred and forty-eight meters (708 yards) into the sky, consisting of one hundred and one stories. By 2015, the audacious building project "Moscow City" was to be completed. About seventy percent of the capital in the Russian Federation is concentrated in Moscow, which, like all world cities, is in motion night and day, and whose gaudy lights forever blink, signaling its importance, much like Las Vegas.

After a conference that ended before lunch, we looked for a restaurant in a hotel; for in 1994 there were not as many good international restaurants in Moscow as there were later, by the dozen, at the end of the nineties. We stopped in front of a classy-looking hotel, the Renaissance Moscow, and entered into the restaurant. To his surprise, Dominik saw a good friend of his sitting alone at a table and introduced me to this friendly man. It turned out to be the world-famous violinist Gidon Kremer. I had always supposed him to be Russian, but he is, in fact, a Latvian of German-Jewish extraction. In 1965 Kremer had attended the Moscow Conservatory, where he was a student of David Oistrakh. After that he was a member of the Leningrad Chamber Orchestra. He made his American debut in 1977 and married the pianist Elena Bashkirova in the same year. In 1978 Kremer decided not to return to the USSR. Dominik and I had a good conversation with the world-star whom we so unexpectedly had encountered in Moscow. In 1995 Dominik gave me two compact discs as a Christmas present. One was Mozart's Violin Concerto K. 485, played by Gidon Kremer with the Vienna Philharmonic under Nikolas Harnoncourt. On the label was written, "With my best wishes to Mr. Widmer, Gidon Kremer." The other compact disc, signed by Krystian Zimerman, was Beethoven's Fifth Piano Concerto, the Emperor Concerto, played by the Vienna Philharmonic under Leonard Bernstein.

It then turned out that Dominik Wlodarczak's mother had for many years associated with various internationally famous musicians, some of whom had lived for a while with the Wlodarczaks. When for a time beginning in 2000 I was the president of the Aargau Symphony Orchestra, I attempted through Mrs. Wlodarczak to arrange to have Kremer as a soloist with the orchestra. But he would only come to Aarau if his Baltic orchestra could come.

Cyrille Kisselevsky held ballet to be on the highest rung of Russian culture, followed by theater and the opera. In his unpublished essay (2002), "Is Russia Unforeseeable?", he wrote, among other things, "Ballerinas are veritable goddesses. In the time of the czars they belonged to the court. Nicolas the Second's great love was Ksechinskaia, who finally married the Grand Duke Andrei Vladimirovitch. I had occasion to visit her in Paris. I was ten years old and she was probably eighty. It was Easter, and, as was traditional, my father went to the home of the celebrities of emigration to wish them in person 'a happy feast of the Resurrection.'"

I want to finish this chapter with some further remarks about Russian culture from Cyrille's above-mentioned essay. "My father passed on to me his interest in operas, from which he loved to whistle the best-known melodies. He himself derived his interest from his maternal grandfather, Nikolai Tikhomirov, doctor to Alexander the Third and to Nicholas the Second, who had a box at the Mariinsky and frequently allowed his grandchildren to take advantage of it.

Our parents often sent their children, from the earliest age, to the opera and ballet. Aware of the honor which was granted to them, they behaved themselves well, while bombarding with pertinent questions whoever accompanied them – often a grandfather or grandmother – and all those nearby could attest, while listening distractedly with one ear, to the indulgence of said grandfather.

It follows that Russians know their classics well and bathe in their ambiance from their earliest years. One day, on Old Arbat Street, I saw a teacher make her whole class of six graders kneel in front of Pushkin's house! It is true that the whole country has raised Pushkin to the rank of a demi-god. His poems and essays are known by heart. The alliance between Pushkin's poetry and the musicality of Tchaikovsky produced the masterpiece, 'Eugene Onegin,' an opera of which every melody and every word are on everyone's lips.

And, whatever may be the spectacle, there are always spectators who come with flowers and throw them at the feet of their idols or, more simply, take them back into their own hands. This homage to art is beautiful and moving."

## Chapter 28

## ALFA CEMENT JOINS THE HOLDERBANK GROUP
## 1996–1999

In March, 1996, Cyrille Kisselevsky came to Russia as the leader of the Alfa 2000 Project. Following are his notes. "This project, worked out by Dominik, was intended to modernize the cement works in which Holderbank possessed substantial minority holdings. The modernization was to involve four areas: technology, finances, marketing, and human resources. Jürgen Jäntsch, a technician from Germany with experience in the cement industry, particularly in Eastern Europe, was hired to work on technology, and the afore-mentioned Andrei Malyutin was hired for overseeing finances. As no one could be found to deal with marketing, we delegated this function to the firm Holtec India, a consulting and cement-engineering firm in Delhi in which Holderbank was involved. Cyrille was responsible for human resources.

The Alfa-2000-Project started in Shurovo; after that came Volsk and then Gornosavodsk. Spassk-Dalny was not included, and this significant amount of shares in Spassk was unfortunately sold later on. The bitterly imperative efforts to improve and modernize the factories made it rapidly apparent that Kharif, lacking experience and the knowledge concerning replacement with modern instruments of major importance, was not the right person. Rather than firing him, the project decided in the spring of 1997 to transfer the central administration to Moscow. As Kharif, who lived in Perm, did not want to move to Moscow, he resigned and joined his brother in America. At that point, this was advantageous for Alfa Cement with respect to modernizing and joining with Holderbank. But no one had taken into account that all of the employees in Perm would be unwilling to move to Moscow. For better or for worse, the project had to undertake building up from the bottom a qualified staff and finding new leadership. At the head of Alfa Cement was a certain Evstratov; the second-in-command was a man named Neretin. In August, 1998, a bitter quarrel arose between the president of Volsk Cement, Bakatin, who had connections in high places, and Evstratov, the CEO of Alfa Cement. On August 23, 1991, Vadim Bakatin was appointed by Gorbachev as the head of the secret service, the KGB. As a result of this internal dispute, Cyrille became the vice president of Human Resources and, at the beginning of 1998, the president of Volsk Cement."

It is worthwhile citing once again the aforementioned essay by Cyrille about his reflections on his time in Russia. "I had the opportunity to make the acquaintance of Vadim Bakatin in 1998, when he succeeded me as president of the administrative council of a large industrial enterprise. Bakatin was named head of the KGB by Gorbachev in August, 1991. It was the first time that the organization had been headed by someone who had not risen through its ranks. Bakatin's mission was to destroy the KGB from within. He has, in fact, also edited a volume dedicated to that unheard-of experience, 'The Deliverance from the KGB,' which was published in 1992. During our long conversations while travelling I recall particularly well the following episode: The first thing Bakatin asked for, on taking possession of his office in the Lubjanka, was that they give him the dossier on his grandfather. His grandfather had been arrested in 1938, and everyone in his family believed that he had survived several years after his arrest by the KGB. Imagine the surprise of Vadim Viktorvich on seeing the dossier in his office within an hour of his arrival and on discovering, on leafing through it, that his grandfather had been 'judged' and condemned to death for having served in the White Army and then executed three weeks after being arrested. Imagine the scene: the grandson, 'heir' of an organization that had killed his grandfather discovers this within the first hour of occupying his position. Bakatin received from Gorbachev the order to transmit to the

Americans the plans for the implantation of the microphones with which the new embassy was rigged. That act, carried out promptly, managed to make both Gorbachev and Bakatin unpopular. In the popular consciousness the Americans continued to be the enemy, and to deliver the plans to them was to soil, not to say betray, his country. Bakatin lost his job one hundred and seven days after starting to work."

As regional controller and, later, assistant to Tres, as well as a member of the board of Alfa Cement, Kurt Häfeli described to me his recollections of the complex incorporation of Alfa Cement into the Holderbank group:

"With most acquisitions the incorporation of an enterprise or even an enterprise group into another compound is connected with 'childhood diseases,'; this was the case with the intended step-by-step incorporation of Alfa Cement and its affiliated companies into the Holderbank group. In the case at hand there were also the difficulties of fundamentally different economic systems – capitalism versus a planned economy – and their effects upon administrative leadership as well as upon the training and practice of new staff.

Nonetheless, we were rather surprised at how much good will there was towards change and with the positive attitude most of the staff exhibited in participating in the changes – although not everyone displayed this equally.

After the signing of the contract and the entrance of the International Finance Corporation (IFC) and Baring as financial investors, it was decided to move the holding administration to Moscow. In addition to the purely holding functions, a western-oriented group management structure with central functions was assigned to oversee operations in the areas of technology, marketing, human resources, and financing and controlling.

The western financial investors, who in the meantime had experienced increased business and thus hoped to enlarge their investment portfolio, looked for appropriate premises to carry out their duties.

Fifty positions were established and appropriate personnel recruited. Most of them were coworkers, either recommended by the Alfa-Bank or having other connections to Alfa Cement. The exceptions were the head of human resources, Cyrille Kisselevsky, and the heads of finances and controlling, at first an American with Russian roots and a knowledge of Russian and later a Swiss, Alexander Vogler, with a background of experience at Holderbank.

The likeable Simeon Kharif had worked hard as the general director of Alfa Cement with the new Holderbank connection and decided to sell his shares in Alfa Cement. A rumor arose that he had moved with his daughter to Florida as a rich man. In less than three years, Kharif had changed from a Red Director into a shrewd capitalist and, with his investments in Alfa Cement, was able, after such a short time, to afford a pleasant life in capitalist America, which never would have been possible even after more than thirty years of hard work in the Soviet cement industry.

The newly engaged general director of the Alfa Cement Group came with the best references from a ministry. However, it soon became apparent that he and some other top employees lacked experience in the industry. They were mostly involved in their own interests. This was particularly evident at board meetings, where reports were given in the style common to officials about the development of the holding company (how many chairs were purchased and so forth), with nary a word about the companies from which the shares had been purchased. The management company and its achievements were scarcely acknowledged – this had evidently also happened in western groups – and not paid for their services. No money was present, and no dividends were flowing to the holding."

The capital of the holding company was rapidly dissipated, and after Holderbank, in particular, was not prepared to put money into the expenses of the holding company, reconstruction was required on a large scale, which meant downsizing personnel and replacing the top leadership.

Connected to all this was a new view of the importance of the shares held in companies deemed strategic. Among other things, it was decided that the Gornasavodsk Factory, which was mired in various kinds of difficulties, did not belong to the group of factories considered strategic by Alfa Cement Investments and, therefore, could not be given financial assistance. The director of the factory, who had invested his Gornasavodsk shares in Alfa Cement against shares in the holding company, suggested that this transaction be cancelled with respect to "his" staff, leaving him to find other solutions for maintaining the factory. This suggestion was accepted by the other shareholders in the holding company. According to several reports, the director would be able to keep the factory going – just how was not known to us.

At that time I was also particularly involved in the introduction of the Holderbank accounting and reporting systems, which, among other things, had to make possible consolidating a combine. This undertaking brought me into contact with the Chief Financial Officers (CFOs) and the staff working most closely with the leadership of the two companies, Shurovo and Volsk. As was usual in states belonging to the former east bloc, these functions were carried out by somewhat older and already heavy-set, but always carefully attired, women. In accord with the Holderbank approach, we put on the table the new system, but not until the factory leadership explained how functions had been implemented under their system, up to the present. We were surprised, initially, to learn that there were two different systems: a planning system and an actual system. It was almost impossible to compare the two systems. It never became clear to us how the planning was to be controlled. It was very hard for us to comprehend the economic planning that supposedly met standards of accountancy, but we could see that it would take time and great effort on the part of our partners to understand and use our western system. Yet we always found that there was good will towards working together.

In particular, visits to Volsk were always an "experience." I have already described in detail the hardships of traveling in the interior of Russia in winter – and when I think back, it seems always to have been in winter. The requisite drinking that accompanied every toast to guests, coworkers, friends, family, women, and so forth have been mentioned already. I especially remember two experiences in Volsk, which Dominik asked me to include.

During one of our winter trips to Volsk, I suddenly had a bad toothache. A few weeks earlier, while repairing a back tooth, my dentist had warned me: "This tooth is a risk; the next time you have a toothache an extraction will be unavoidable. Wouldn't you rather have this done right away, or would you rather have it repaired one more time?" I refused the option of extraction; the reader can probably guess why. Now I had to face this unpleasant procedure in the heart of Russia.

The Volsk factory was well furnished with facilities that were not strictly necessary, such as a gymnasium, a sauna, and a sick room. The sick room was staffed by a few nurses and a jovial factory doctor, whom I knew from social occasions and innumerable toasts. The head of the factory, whom I asked about a local dentist, directed me to the factory doctor, who took me to the city dental clinic. This was a plain structure with several stories, looking like an administration building, where more than twenty fellow sufferers sat in the reception area. The factory doctor took care of the admission formalities for me, and to my relief, but also to my embarrassment, I was taken directly past everyone else waiting in the waiting area of the extraction unit. The clinic was clearly divided into units, such as x-rays, general dental examinations, fillings, extractions, and so forth, each having its own doctor. Here, too, was a waiting room full of people. Before entering this room, one had to remove one's shoes and put on felt slippers. Here I was again given a chair as the first in line, while the others bore their waiting very stoically. Soon my predecessor appeared in the doorway with a red face, and the very robust-appearing female dental assistant directed me to the treatment chair, which was very similar to the chair I remembered from my first visit to the dentist, about fifty years ago. I made a hash of things right away with the terrifying dental assistant by asking her in sign language to take away the enamel bowl containing, like trophies, the teeth that had presumably been pulled that morning, as they were almost making me sick.

After a doubtless pleasant exchange of words between the lady dentist (who was as buxom as her assistant) and the official factory dentist, who also acted as the translator, my situation was described. A quick look in the mouth and then the question if an x-ray had already been taken; a pulled tooth, after all, was an irredeemable loss, and, as such, should be carefully considered.

This entailed a switch to the x-ray department: passing by the fellow sufferers in the waiting room, taking off the felt slippers, putting on the winter shoes, going downstairs to the x-ray department, taking off the shoes, putting on the felt slippers, walking past the people waiting at the entrance to the x-ray room, having the x-ray taken, back through the waiting room to the shoe depository, felt slippers off, winter boots on, up the stairs, winter boots off, felt slippers on, through the waiting room past the fellow sufferer, who had in the meantime moved up by one chair and was not necessarily looking understanding, and to the first chair in front of the entrance to the "torture chamber."

Here, too, it was not long until I could again sit on the ominous chair on which treatment would be delivered and was told that the tooth could really not be saved. So I was given a shot, a few minutes after which I could feel almost no difference. Even after the second shot, my lips were scarcely numb – either the questionable medications in Russia were very weak or the situation made me insensitive. The dentist, with the figure of a babushka-clad peasant, could not understand, at any rate, why I was not reacting and did not want to waste any more time. She gestured to her assistant, who weighed some one hundred kilos, that she should hold my head tightly while she went to work. I felt almost as though my head was being torn off – in an attempt to restrain me from fleeing the agonizing torture they were inflicting, if such was my plan.

Following the implementation of *the* treatment, the exchange of shoes, and the frenzied flight from the extraction unit, I was driven back to the sick room at the factory, where I was given more pain killers. My blood pressure was extraordinarily high and, for me, absolutely out of range, causing the factory doctor to keep me in the sick room for observation. But the next day all was in order, and I could continue with my work. The comment of my dentist in Switzerland was simply that it was not unusual for a patient's blood pressure to skyrocket when he performed extractions.

I have much more pleasant memories of another visit to Volsk, this time in summer. A Holderbank delegation under the newly-appointed Director of Investments in Russia, was given an orientation to the factory, particularly to its progress and to the plans for integration into the Alfa Cement group and Holderbank. As the visit fell on a weekend, the visitors were offered something special. The Volsk Factory owned a tugboat which was clearly no longer being used for its original purpose but instead for expeditions on the river. In any case, it had been freshly painted, and appeared to be quite seaworthy. After traveling along the river, a waterway which looked to me as wide as Lake Hallwil in Switzerland, we reached a small island, where we were able to have our midday meal outside, as the boat was generously stocked with plenty of drinks and picnic baskets. The return trip found everyone in high spirits and reflected the warm and amiable character of our Russian hosts. Still today, I look forward to even a short boat trip on the Volga, as I had experienced it before such trips had become so popular with west European tourists, an attraction that continues to draw them to.

## Chapter 29

## THE YEARS 1998 TO 2000

Since, as I mentioned already, I left the administrative council of Alfa Cement in mid-1998, I called on another witness, besides Cyrille Kisselevsky and Kurt Häfeli. I asked Alexander Vogler, the chief financial officer of Alfa Cement from 1998 to 2000, to tell me about his experiences and further developments in Russia, particularly in Alfa Cement, during the period of his tenure.

Alexander Vogler wrote me as follows: "Before my first visit to Russia, I had accompanied the Holcim acquisitions in Bulgaria and Rumania as the group controller. Thus I thought working in Russia would not be too demanding.

In December 1997 I was given the assignment of doing a due diligence in Uzbekistan, a former Soviet republic. This was the first time that I was confronted with the problem of bartering, the business of swapping. As in the course of my work I walked through the warehouse, I discovered in a side room a huge heap of boxes. When I asked what was in them, it was explained that they contained light-bulbs, the result of a barter exchange. Shortly thereafter I found that because of incorrect storage – the cold wind blowing through broken windows – the desert sands had torn open the cartons and even broken the glass in some of the bulbs. Back in bookkeeping, I learned that this barter deal had been made by the former head of sales who, unfortunately, had departed this life two weeks before our visit. As was disclosed to me under pressure, he had made this arrangement involuntarily. The partially damaged bulbs have not yet been assessed and, I was told, that it would take at least two years before the undamaged bulbs could be used.

So I was forewarned by my experience in Uzbekistan and was subsequently able to determine that the further the cement factory was from Moscow, the greater the role played by barter. In Volsk, for instance, cigarettes and sausages were found in the inventory. With the cigarettes, there was a bigger discrepancy between the inventory report and the actual stock, stemming from 'natural' disappearance – that is, from theft.

In winter, 1998, I was sent with colleagues to Moscow for a due diligence. It concerned the possible acquisition of Stern Cement. Here one must know that this group in the western part of Russia held shares in which Alfa Cement also had smaller shares. Our people were familiar with the technical details of the factories. This effort was supported by an international company for economic inspection. Here, too, the financial problems were quickly isolated: barter arrangements and taxes that were out of balance. After a brief analysis, Tres Pestalozzi decided to discontinue the due diligence, as the possible costs for acquisition bore no relation to the costs for maintenance and taxes.

In June, 1998, after a visit to a seminar in Switzerland, I got a call from my superior Thomas Aebischer, now CFO of Holcim and member of the Executive Committee, informing me that the CFO of Alfa Cement had decided to leave after just one year. He explained further that after the seminar I should meet with Kurt Häfeli in Jona to receive a briefing about the situation of the group. In Jona, then, I met with two future colleagues: one was the projected technical head and the other the projected CFO of the Volsk factory. We were joined briefly at this meeting by the successor of Tres Pestalozzi, who in the meantime had taken over from Tres the position of a member of the Executive Committee responsible for Europe.

We expected to visit Moscow, Shurovo, and Volsk in July, 1998. I will never forget the two days in Volsk, and for two reasons: first, because this visit was distinguished by a presentation by the factory head, Victor Semenindeykin, in which an enormous number of gold teeth flashed when he opened his mouth, and second, because of an agreeable expedition on the Volga. The friendly head of the factory had prepared a pleasant presentation in which he essentially proposed which capital expenditures (CAPEX) should be made. The new member of the Executive Committee for Europe (successor of Pestalozzi) simply asked if these investments were to be made from the factory's cash flow. I will also not forget the bewildered face made by Victor, who had probably heard the term 'cash flow' for the first time that day. The colleagues from Alfa Cement Moscow were slightly embarrassed. The new European head made the witty comment, 'Holderbank is not a bank.' How true – and this remark was important later on when the name Holderbank was changed to Holcim.

Victor epitomized for me the thinking of an amiable Soviet technocrat. In the past one sent the investment plan to the ministry; Moscow then sent the means. Before the collapse of the USSR, much of the money in Saratov Oblast went to the military, as there were important airports and rocket silos in this province. Looking at the plants that were possible competitors of the Volsk factory, we were shocked to discover that all plants were working to capacity. In order to get cash, the factories had to make deliveries in far-off Moscow, whereby they of course delivered cement to the home market of Shurovo.

Now the good Victor was confronted for the first time with cash flow and production costs. It was high time and long overdue that he had an experienced technical leader and finance director at his side.

After this stressful meeting, Victor became friendly. The trip on the Volga was wonderful. The fish we were served tasted excellent. Only after a swim in the Volga did I begin to think things over. I was wearing a Swatch watch on my wrist and kept it on during our swim. After the swim, I noticed that the Plexiglas cover over the dial was smeared with a film! I was told that there were many industrial sites along the Volga; even though they were no longer in full production, there was still a good deal of untreated pollution in these waters.

The small city of Volsk, lying on the Volga between Samara and Saratov, got its first little cement factory in 1897. After the October Revolution the owner was dispossessed, and the factory was renamed 'Red October.' Later a larger plant was added, named 'Bolshevik.' When, in September 1998, in Moscow, I was appointed to the CFO Group of Alfa Cement, we concentrated on restructuring the group. On paper, the Alfa Cement Group looked impressive because of its size, but there was no synergy among the factories under its aegis, especially with respect to their markets and technically meaningful coordinated work. The cash flow of the companies was insufficient, and, frequently, there were interruptions in production because necessary maintenance work could not be performed, the firm lacking sufficient liquid assets.

We had analyzed the situation at our discussions in Moscow and had come to the conclusion that, with the closing of the small Red October Factory in Volks, employment in the larger Bolshevik Factory could be improved. This could also lead to optimizing the selling price attainable for its product. Naturally we were also aware of the social components, and proposed that this had to be done with due consideration to such personnel. Suitable discussions were held at the site and, of course, this idea quickly made the rounds.

The head of the Bolshevik Factory at Volsk was called to Saratov by the Governor of Saratov Oblast (Province), Dmitry Ayatskov, to explain the situation to him; and a delegation, of which the President of Volsk, Vadim Bakatin, was a member, flew in from Moscow. Bakatin had been the Minister of the Interior under Gorbachev (1988–1990) and was the last chairman of the

KGB (1990); in 1991 he ran against Yeltsin for the presidency. For him, too, it was difficult to understand the economic connection, but in the end he supported the project.

The small cement factory also included a limestone factory. When the Moscow delegation met with Governor Ayatskov, he yelled, 'I will not allow the only limestone factory in my province to close. I will have it taken over by the state!' After months of back and forth negotiations, we finally had to drop the project, as there was too much pressure from the local government.

Ayatskov was an *apparatchik* who had had no great career prospects in the old Soviet era. With the downfall of the Soviet government, he had cleverly managed to be nominated vice-mayor of Saratov, and in 1996 he was named governor of the Saratov Oblast.

The year 1998 brought decisive changes with the August crisis. [See the following chapter.] At that time the Group consolidated four cement plants (Shurovo, Volsk, Gornosavodsk, and Spassk) and possessed some minority shares. For instance, it had minority shares in plants belonging to the Stern Group. As it did not acquire the Stern Group, these minority shares were useless and also yielded no profits. At the beginning there were some skirmishes concerning the rights of shareholders, but in the end we gave up these shares.

Some of the most important minority shares were derived from the Novoros Cement Factory, a plant located in Novorossiysk, a city of approximately two hundred and fifty thousand inhabitants, situated on the Black Sea and representing Russia's most important harbor. As a result of the Russian-Turkish War, the coastline ceased to be under the control of the Ottoman Empire, but fell to Russia instead. (In ancient times there was a Greek colony on the banks of Tsemess Bay.) The Novorossiysk region is one of Russia's most important wine districts. The Abrau-Dyurso vineyards were established in 1870 by Alexander the Third. They produce table and sparkling wines for local consumption. Novoros Cement exports cement to Spain, the Dominican Republic, Turkey, Italy, and Egypt. Holders of shares in Novoros Cement, though invested sufficiently to qualify as a majority, were stymied in their attempts to gain this recognition by a former member of the KGB who, somehow, controlled the reins of power. It was to take time for shares in Novoros to bloom. Today the plant that supports the value of these shares is flourishing; and the construction for the Olympics and Formel-1-Course in Sochi will see the profits grow still greater. Novoros Cement made so much money that the company was able to purchase the cement companies of Inteko from Elena Baturina (wife of the major of Moscow) on July 4, 2011. The factories in question were those they had acquired after the sale to Eurocement.

Shurovo, with the Moscow market, had certainly the most attractive market potential. The competition in the Moscow market in 1998–2000 was fierce, as many factories made deliveries in the Moscow cash market. One of Vladimir Putin's most important decrees was outlawing bartering.

What happened to Spassk Cement? Because it was eight time zones away from Moscow, it was hard to control the management. Certainly the nearby Chinese market was attractive, but huge investments were necessary, and, as usual, no liquid assets were available. In the end it proved possible to sell the factory to an investment company. It was advantageous for the buyer, while for Alfa Cement it meant the freeing up of important resources.

So then Alfa Cement had only Gornosavodsk, where everything had begun, and Volsk and Shurovo. One of the minority shareholders of Alfa Cement was Vadim Furman. He was the head of the Gornosavodsk factory and had at one time become important under Kharif. At an administrative meeting of Alfa Cement, he made a very emotional speech in which he proposed exchanging his Alfa Cement shares for Gornosavodsk shares. This proposal was accepted. And today he is still the head of this factory, which principally does business with Yekaterinburg.

Thus the future of the Alfa Group came to an end; that is, the one-time-on-paper largest cement group in Russia shrank down to just two plants, Shurovo and Volsk! The whole process was not without emotion and was not always understood by my Russian colleagues. The situation changed completely after Tres withdrew. Now we had to buy time.

But how were we to finance the mid-term investments? In 1999 we turned to the European Bank for Reconstruction and Development (EBRD) and IFC to secure financing, via Holderbank. EBRD refused us immediately. IFC wanted to perform a technical due diligence before undertaking further steps. In December 1999, IFC told us they might be able to furnish financing, but only if Holderbank were the first strategic investor. It came down to waiting to see if the situation in Russia would change.

When I came to Moscow in 1998, Alfa Cement had rented a modern office building within sight of the Hotel Ukraine and the White House on the banks of the Moscow River. After all, it was at the time the largest cement group in Russia. The administration of the Alfa Cement Holding Company had about fifty employees. After Cyril Kisselevsky returned to Switzerland, I stayed on in Russia, the only expat in the holding company. As a result of budgetary economies and the shrinking number of employees on staff at the factories in Shurovo and Volsk, the number of personnel at Alfa Holding, by the end of 2000, was reduced to about six employees.

Some of the eastern European countries had an easier time with privatization than Russia, or they gave themselves more time. But the distinctive concept of privatization as it occurred in Russia could not be avoided: corruption and the rearranging of what once belonged to the state at the expense of the populace. Public sale with the advice of EBRD was one option, as was done in Rumania, for instance. This kind of privatization also leaves a bitter after-taste. Insider privatization such as took place in Russia let loose a new group of oligarchs. The false strategy of privatization, a policy enacted without transparency, had the effect of unduly prolonging the necessary reform process. In the mid-nineties, the Russian cement market had a large excess capacity. The factories somehow managed to muddle along. Factories situated in secondary market areas did not have to fear great changes of owners. Other factories, located near Moscow, came under the ownership of persons and groups that controlled enterprises in various other areas which were money machines.

After I left Russia and Holderbank, I worked for several years in Switzerland for a Russian investor who had made his money in aluminum. He had first worked as the leading manager for an oligarch who had, within a decade, worked his way up from being simply a minister of one region to being a multi-millionaire. It became clear to me that there had been a time in which these business people had been in direct confrontation with the underworld. I got the impression that relatively early on some of those who are now well-known oligarchs had already made agreements as to who would take over which industry. Most important, of course, were oil, aluminum, and metal, all the areas in which Russia played a significant part in the world market. All other areas, those confined to internal markets, were allowed to become free enterprises, but as soon as they became profitable they aroused the envy of the oligarchs or the mafia. It remains to be seen if Russia can really be transformed into an economy which goes beyond a dependency on raw materials, an economy that makes the country vulnerable to the ups and downs of world market prices".

## Chapter 30

## THE FINANCIAL CRISIS
## 1998

The venerable Moscow journalist Roman Berger, cited previously, wrote the following in a critical article.

"While in the middle of the nineties the rest of Russia was at risk of falling into depression, the spirit of a gold rush reigned in Moscow. The stock market was booming. The boom rested on money that was in the country only briefly and quickly made a profit. At the same time the otherwise weary state covered household deficits with short-term loans with interest as great as two hundred percent. The state-backed loans developed into a pyramid scheme. On August 17, 1998, just a few days after President Yeltsin had promised that there would be no devaluation, the ruble collapsed and with it most of the large banks. The system of state loans and enormous speculation fell apart. After the hyperinflation, the August crisis hit the growing middle class the hardest, that is, the very class of the population that should have been the most important basis for democracy and a free market economy." Berger continued. "August 1998 revealed the true character of privatization which placed capital in the hands of an 'elite,' who did not increase values but rather skimmed off the profits and for the most part sent them out of the country. This was also the case with the Growth Index Fund (IWF). According to the estimates of the New York Times (August 15, 1999), between two hundred and five hundred billion US dollars flowed out of Russia between 1993 and 1998. In hearings in the American congress, highly placed government officials and experts described this drain of capital as a 'gigantic plunder of Russia' under the protection of international financial institutions and 'an infusion of blood for the western financial world.'

In the meantime Russia had reimbursed the credit, thanks to petro-dollars. The same credits which in the nineties had disappeared into the pockets of the new Russian cleptocracy and American as well as European banks now were repaid from the state stability funds. That is to say, the Russian people paid the bill."

The difficult days of the 1998 financial crisis ended in virtual state bankruptcy, but Russia recovered with astonishing rapidity from the so-called ruble crisis. A mixture of willingness to reform and luck laid the foundations for a long period of growth. Russia was able to build upon the market economic foundations laid in the nineteen nineties (Neue Zurcher Zeitung, September 7, 2011).

## Chapter 31

## CONSOLIDATION OF THE RUSSIAN CEMENT INDUSTRY 1994–2011

In May, 1994, through minority shares of nineteen percent with Alfa Cement, Holderbank had shares in the following cement factories: Gornosavodsk (60 percent), Novoros (42 percent), and Suchoi Log (18.6 percent), and also, with smaller shares, in Volsk and Shurovo. With the money it invested in Alfa Cement, Holderbank, within a year, was also able to buy majority shares in Spassk (60 percent) and Shurovo (65 Percent) With these holdings, Alfa Cement was the largest cement group in Russia in 1995.

In 1998 I left the Board of Directors of Alfa Cement for reasons connected to the premature and voluntary departure of Tres Pestalozzi from the Holderbank Executive Committee and the switch to his successor. Holderbank subsequently sold various shares and became majority stockholders in Shurovo and Volsk. These sales have already been commented upon by Alexander Vogler.

Stern purchased in rapid succession four cement factories: Maltsovsky (1995), Mikhailov (1996), Lipetsk (1997), and Savinsky (2001).

Dyckerhof Cement was the majority stockholder in Suchoi Log in the Urals.

Lafarge was able to buy majority shares in Voskresenk, near Moscow, in 1996. In 2003 it also acquired Ural Cement.

In 2002, Heidelberg purchased majority shares in Slancy, near St. Petersburg.

In 1991 Yelena Baturina, the richest woman in Russia and the wife of the all-powerful mayor of Moscow, Juri Luschkov, founded in 1991 the Russian enterprise Inteko, which initially dealt in synthetic materials and then went into construction in Russia. In the following years the company obtained many contracts in the city of Moscow such as the construction of the eighty-five thousand seat Olympic Stadium Luschniki.

Inteko purchsed Podgorensky Tsement and Oskoi Tsement in 2002. In 2003 it purchased Belgorodsky Tsement, and in 2004 it purchased shares in Pikalevsky Tsement and minority shares in Zhigulevsk and Ulyanovsk, as well as a factory in the Ukraine. In the meantime Inteko showed a cement capacity of fourteen million tons. In 2005 Inteko – that is to say, Yelena Baturina – made the strategic decision to sell all its cement shares, which had been integrated into the construction company Inteko. Yet even after the sale of the cement works, Inteko remained the largest construction enterprise in Russia. In April 2005, Inteko's cement plants were taken over by Eurocement. This group, controlled by Filaret Galtchev, already had an annual cement capacity of 7.5 million tons through the purchase of the Stern group. Thus Eurocement had in 2005 a total cement capacity of 21.5 million tons, giving it more than forty percent of the Russian market. The enterprise is active in Russia, as well in the Ukraine and in Uzbekistan, employing a total of thirty thousand people.

In January 2004 Alfa Cement, with a capacity of 4.1 million tons of cement, became a branch of Holcim, operating as a branch of the "Holcim Foreign Shares Participation Ltd.". The important shares – Gornosavodsk, in the Urals, Novoros, on the Black Sea, and Spassk, in far eastern Russia, in the meantime, had been sold or traded with Alfa Cement for packets of shares.

Inteko purchased cement shares again in 2006, this time in Verkhnebakansky and Atakai Tsement. In September 2008, the

Russian Eurocement Combine took some greater risks and purchased, in two steps, shares of 6.25 percent in the Swiss cement combine Holcim! We asked ourselves if Holcim would in time become a Russian-controlled company.

In September 2011, the major stockholder Eurocement increased its holdings to 10.1 percent. The result: Russia wants to come to Europe, this time without tanks. Eurocement at the gates? In response, Thomas Schmidheiny (main shareholder of Holcim) increased his Holcim's holdings from 18.2 to 20 percent. The newspapers reported that both Schmidheiny and the Russians bought advantageously (less than the book rate).

As the majority stockholder, Thomas Schmidheiny controlled the Holcim group until 2003. After the introduction of Bearer shares instead of Registered shares (with more voting power), his voice was reduced by half, from fifty-four to twenty-seven percent. In the following years his share sank to 18.2 percent.

The "Tagesanzeiger" (Swiss Newspaper) of December 10, 2011, established the following, among other things: "Since Filaret Galtchev, owner of Russia's largest cement combine, Eurocement, increased his shares in Holcim to ten percent, there is speculation about his intentions. Is he, as insinuated in the Financial Times, at war with Holcim's major shareholder, Thomas Schmidheiny, who recently increased his holdings to twenty percent? In the summer of 2007, in the middle of the market boom, Holcim was worth over forty billion francs. Since then, the value of its holdings has dropped to seventeen billion francs and thus is worth sizably less than the book value quoted in the mid-year report. Galtchev clearly saw Holcim as a good catch and made a strong purchase. But the Swiss cement giant is probably too much for a takeover by him. With assets of 3.5 billion US dollars, Galtchev is only thirty-first on the Forbes List of Russia's Richest. Oerlikon's major shareholder, Victor Vekselberg, with thirteen billion, is in tenth place.

But who is the owner, almost unknown here, of Eurocement, which with sixteen factories and a 37.5 million ton capacity is the largest cement producer in Russia? Galtchev, the mining engineer, grew rich by working with and exporting coal and then buying up one cement factory after another, sometimes in combination with the oligarch Abramovitz, with whom he later quarreled.

Like many Russian oligarchs, Galtchev financed his rise largely on credit. Last year he was in debt to Sberbank alone for forty-nine billion rubles (1.4 billion francs). No one knows how secure his cement combine is. That Filaret Galtchev stocked up on Holcim shares indicates that, like many wealthy Russians, he wants to shelter his assets from state takeovers. Galtchev's holdings in Zürich, to which he added in 2007 his cement shares in Russia, Uzbekistan, and the Ukraine, amounted to a share capital of four hundred and thirty million francs."

Opening of the completely modernized and enlarged Shurovo-Cement plant of Holcim in the summer 2011.
Right: the Russian President Medvedev, in the middle: the Swiss President Calmy-Rey and besides Holcim CEO Akermann. Foto: Holcim

## Chapter 32

## RUSSIA TODAY AND TOMORROW

Thanks to rising prices in oil, Russia has grown from being a washed-out successor to the Soviet Union to being a relative strong capitalist country. While many people still today, twenty years later, mourn for the bygone Soviet Union, many young people know Marx and Lenin only as street names. Russia has experienced a remarkable economic boom in going from a planned to a market economy. Among the BRIC states, the four fastest growing economies (Brazil, Russia, India, and China), Russia is the geographically largest state with the highest per capita income of 15,900 US dollars. According to the Central Intelligence Agency's "World Fact Book," that is greater than fifty percent more than the per capita income in Brazil and twice the size of that in China. The number of families in Russia with an annual income of more than ten thousand US dollars has tripled in the last three years. A strong capitalist state with the third largest reserve in assets has arisen from an economically depressed empire. To be sure, this development started about ten years ago. As recently as 1998 Russia was faced with bankruptcy. The economic advance followed largely in the period in which Vladimir Putin was president, 2000 to 2008 (Neue Zürcher Zeitung (NZZ), November 7, 2011).

As the NZZ announced on Sunday (June 5, 2011), the Russian economy took another step. The sheer size of Russia makes is an interesting market for Swiss enterprises. In 2010, Russian exports equaled 2.7 billion Swiss francs. Yet in spite of everything, business with Russia followed its own rules. Still today nothing happens without *connections*. The seats of power are in Moscow, as in Soviet days. Complicated customs regulations interfere with exports. The economy remains strongly based in raw materials and energy, items that subject it to the vicissitudes of the world market. Many businesses develop out of those that had existed in Soviet days. When it comes to technology, most businesses limp along behind businesses elsewhere. The need for investment is enormous, while the costs of modernization are frighteningly high.

As indicated in a press release of Holcim dated July 13, 2011, Holcim showed an increase of fifteen percent in cement in Russia in 2011 and in India an increase of eight to ten percent. It also announced the opening of a new and completely modernized cement plant in Shurovo (one hundred kilometers from Moscow). This plant has an annual capacity of 2.1 million tons and was opened in the presence of Russian President Dimitri Medvedev and Swiss President Micheline Calmy-Rey. Dominik and I were of course happy to hear this, but this announcement gave us pause, given our original goals for acquisitions in Russia. According to the press release, Holcim expects that the Russian cement market will in five to ten years increase from a volume of eighty to one hundred million tons. Today it stands at fifty-seven million tons. As the CEO explained, "We are active in this market and hold shares of ten to fifteen percent. Thus we are about number four. The Shurovo factory can be sure of providing long-term service with high-quality construction material in the greater Moscow area." President Dimitri Medvedev stated in his welcoming address, "This plant is the advertisement of the Russian cement industry and sets new standards for environmental friendliness."

However, the stated investment sum of five hundred million Euros for construction and modernization strikes me as extremely high. Given the prospect of long-term positive development in Russia, I cannot see why, after the departure of Tres Pestalozzi from the leadership of the combine in 1998, the many shares in interesting factory positions were sold, for about the price of a sandwich, or traded against Alfa-Cement shares. Of course, at the time, it was difficult to get additional money from Holcim for building up minority shares in factories of Alfa Cement. With some courage and a far-sighted view of the Russian potential, it really ought to have been clear that, instead of the sale of the minority shares, additional shares in their own cement plants could have been purchased, so that Holcim would control these factories. If that had been done, Holcim would now be the largest or at least the second largest cement producer in Russia. Later, of course, a lot of money would have had to been spent for the rehabilitation of these plants, but important positions would have been filled by Holcim. Above all, had these additional expenditures been committed as suggested, Holcim would be today a sufficient counter-balance in the home market to Galtchev (Eurocement). Had Holcim seized fully the opportunities present in Russia during the post-Soviet period of the nineties, by paying for improvements in existing factories or by creating new factories, such additional outlays of money, by today's investment standards, would have yielded handsome dividends and create a model of minimizing risk in the field of partnerships-with-foreign- companies by applying certain precautions. Holcim's timid approach to ground-floor investment opportunities that had existed in Russia's newly privatized economy represents, in my opinion, the loss of the last window of opportunity to partner with an industry promising lucrative rewards.

Back to Russia today and yesterday. According to the NZZ (June 15, 2011), glaringly apparent riches are to be seen in the Russian capital: dark Maybach limousines and conspicuous Hummer vehicles parked in front of expensive and glittering restaurants are part of the daily picture of the city. These sights are generally rounded out with security people, who are more a status symbol than a necessity.

Since 2011, Russia has belonged, along with China and the USA, to the exclusive club of the countries with more than one hundred billionaires: Russia has one hundred and one of these very wealthy people. Their age is striking: the average age of these billionaires is forty-nine, while in other countries it is sixty to seventy-four. Their wealth is of a later date: the number grew from seven in 2002 to twenty-seven in 2005. At the beginning of 2011 the approximately one hundred billionaires in Russia possessed among them assets of about four hundred and thirty-two billion US dollars. According to the consulting firm Deloitte, the assets of the millionaires will increase from the present collective sum of seventy-nine million US dollars to two thousand seven hundred billion US dollars in 2020.

According to an article in the NZZ (September 6, 2011), the standard of living has steadily risen since the beginning of the new century and the presidency of Vladimir Putin. Thanks to the high income derived from the export of gas and oil, Moscow has become a luxurious metropolis with the highest concentration of billionaires in the world and has corresponding astronomical prices. Even the slowly expanding middle class has profited from economic growth and the booming service sector, but rural areas are excluded from this progress. While the cities are flourishing, the outlying surroundings are losing population. After the collapse of the Soviet Union, agricultural production remained at the bottom for a long time. Privatization succeeded only slowly, and the allocation of credit came to a halt. Russia, the country with the largest per capita area of arable land, had to import even grain. Since then, agriculture, which is largely organized into large cooperatives, has recovered. There are hardly any small or medium-sized family enterprises. Thus large areas of this huge land are gradually dying out.

Compared to the crisis with debt in many western states, Russia appears stable. In contrast to 2009, the debts of the banks and enterprises are less than in 2009. The low governmental debt quota is less than ten percent of the GDP; most industrial countries could only dream of this. In addition, Russia has today the third greatest reserve of foreign currency. The outlook for growth is intact; the international currency fund is plus 4.8 percent for Russia. To be sure, Russia experienced a decline in the GDP of 7.9 percent in 2009, but this number is small in relation to the average rate of 7 percent during the years 2000 to 2007. None of the other BRIC states were hit as hard as Russia. Given the background of the European debt crisis and the risks of a global economic weakening, a further decline in growth (then over four percent) in the coming years is possible, but the outlook for growth is nonetheless intact. Even if the predicted growth of something over four percent for Russia in the next few years is small, the country is doing well compared to other industrial nations. In the long run, the rise in consumption and the growth of the middle class will be the most significant reasons for the increase. Consumption accounts for about fifty percent of the gross national product. In industrial countries this figure is about sixty percent.

The Growth Index Fund recommends reducing the fiscal dependence on oil, decreasing inflation, establishing a competitive banking system, and improving the basic conditions for economic investment and diversification. At present, the price of oil, such as is found in the Urals, is more than one hundred US dollars a barrel. If this declined to eighty US dollars, economic growth for 2012 would be just two percent instead of just four percent. If the price were sixty US dollars, Russia would sink into a recession (NZZ, October 10, 2011).

Almost twenty years after the end of the Soviet Union, society is presumably freer than ever before in the history of Russia for private development, even if the economic or social rise is limited for many in the middle generation. The political boundaries have remained stricter (NZZ, May 7, 2011).

Considering that despite the euphoria that ensued following the collapse of the Soviet state at the beginning of the nineties people were suddenly forced to take responsibility for themselves, this enormous transition from a planned to a market economy was, in the end, quite successful. The fear that it released an overwhelming sense of helplessness has disappeared today and has been replaced by creative forces. Fortunately no one today believes in the state as the all-encompassing provider.

It may nonetheless be true, as stated in NZZ (August 20–21, 2012), that there is still a rigid hierarchy running the country: a small group of politicians, officers, secret agents, and business people (nomenclatura). All of the elements of a living democracy that do not consist solely in a formal election that were realized after the August, 1991, putsch were partially or altogether abolished. Voting rights were altered, and independent representatives disappeared, as did the liberal parties in opposition.

I do think it is questionable whether we in Switzerland are justified in measuring and qualifying other states according to our ideals of (direct) democracy. Russia has at least economically and also politically made giant steps forward and is beginning to become a true partner of the west.

The potential is great but it is not being used fully. The "Russia Competitiveness Report 2011," presented by the Sberbank and the World Economic Forum, speaks to this point regarding Russia's ability to compete. The authors stress the fact that Russia, with the greatest land mass in the world, has fallen behind China, India, and Brazil because its productivity has not increased. With its one hundred and forty-three million inhabitants, Russia could have clear competitive advantages, given the size of its market, the plentitude of well-educated people, and the wealth of natural resources.

Of course, setbacks keep recurring. At the moment (2011), Russian currency is weaker than it has been for years. The curve of the stock market, too, is pointing downwards. Because of the protracted European debt crisis and the fear of a worldwide recession, the price of oil is depressed, which has serious effects on Russia. In addition, Moscow is fighting the flight of capital (NZZ, September 24, 2011).

The European Union is by far Russia's biggest trading partner, and the volume of business has grown rapidly over the last decade. In 2010 almost half of Russia's export business came from the European Union; the volume of business between 2000 and 2010 grew from sixty-six to an amazing three hundred billion US dollars – that is, it quadrupled. The Russian per capita income increased almost ten-fold in the past decade, reaching fifteen thousand nine hundred US dollars. According to the newest Human Development Index Report of the United Nations, Russia is "a developed land with average income."

Enterprises in Western Europe react to the increase in disposable income by turning to Russia and profiting from the rapidly growing consumer market. Russia, so it is alleged, is becoming one of the largest automobile markets in the next five years.

In an article about Pepsi, "Bullish on Russia," the Financial Times (October 10, 2011) wrote: "There are some groups that seem to be perfectly content about the country's political and fiscal direction. Take for instance Pepsico. Over the last decade, the company has invested USD 19 billion in Russia, thanks to a close working relationship with the Kremlin leadership. And over the next two years, under Putin's leadership, the company will invest an additional USD one billion dollars, Indra Nooyi, Pepsico's chief executive, said in Moscow on Monday after a meeting between Putin and global business leaders. Speaking to journalists at a separate event after the meeting, Nooyi said Pepsico was unperturbed by Putin's return to power. "The politics of Russia is not what worries us," she said in response to a question from **beyondbrics** (a forum for guest contributions of the Financial Times): "We worry whether the leadership is friendly to investment and I can tell you that over the last few decades the leadership has been friendly to Pepsi. And we've had a great record with them whether it is building plants, whether it is helping us through regulations and licenses to put in a potato crop, the Russian government has worked very constructively with us. And that's what matters to us. Russia's fundamentals are very good. It's a great base of oil, natural resources. It's got all the basic requirements to be a successful country for the long term,' she added."

The NZZ of August 10, 2011 states that the post-Soviet territory is again in a state of transition. In St. Petersburg eight members of the Commonwealth of Independent States (CIS) have signed an agreement for free trade; Uzbekistan, Turkmenistan, and Azerbaijan are expected to sign the agreement by the end of 2011. The free enterprise zone will eliminate import and export duties.

The CIS was founded after the breakdown of the Soviet Union in 1991. With the exception of the Baltic States and Georgia, all the successor states of the Soviet Union are represented. Russia had already formed a customs union with White Russia and Kazakhstan, which signified a deeper integration rather than just a free trade zone.

Compared to other big emerging markets, Russia limps along behind other such developing countries on the Index of Foreign Direct Investments (FDI). According to the financial ministry, the country received about fourteen billion US dollars FDI in 2010 and thus significantly less than India, with twenty-six billion US dollars, and China, with a gigantic one hundred and six billion US dollars.

The Russian President Medvedev already has concrete visions for reforms. By August 2011, a radical privatization program is supposed to be adopted and political power is supposed to be decentralized. This privatization program is supposed to bring 58.5 billion US dollars into Russia by the year 2015. More than one thousand firms are supposed to be partially or entirely privatized. A test for the seriousness of this plan will be the projected sale in 2012 of fifteen percent of the oil giant Rosneft, which at present market prices would produce ten billion US dollars. In order to attract investments, limits are to be put on the allowance of Russian paper currency out of the country and restrictions on visas for investors are to be eased.

# Chapter 33

## CONCLUSION

As I have mentioned already, Russia undoubtedly has great potential. Its advantages include easy access to raw materials, the size of the market, and the population's relatively good education in mathematics and the natural sciences. It must also not be forgotten that the Russian Federation is significantly smaller than was the Soviet Union at the end of 1991, yet remains geographically the largest country in the world, almost twice the size of the United States.

My many visits to Russia were rich in experiences that deepened my understanding of the beauty of this enormous country, especially of the thinking of its friendly population, experiences that brought about perceptions in stark contrast to those I had entertained at an earlier period of my life. My military training in Switzerland had impressed upon me the danger of an attack on Western Europe by the Soviet Union, leading to the thinking of the Cold War Era, that a strong army was necessary to save freedom and our well-being. Above all, we viewed the military might of the USA as our life insurance. From being a Cold War Westerner who saw every Russian as a dangerous enemy programmed to believe in and proselytize for a false ideology, I became a friend and in many ways an admirer of the "Russian soul" and culture. Russians are so lovable and hospitable, it is almost smothering. My improved understanding of the land and of the people would have been impossible without my many trips, my contacts with simple workers, the red directors, politicians, bureaucrats, and oligarchs, and my wish to gain greater insight into the Russian past and present. Thus I believe that my Russian experience is in complete agreement with the quote from Kierkegaard which I used to introduce this book: "Life can only be *understood* by looking backwards, but it must be *lived* by looking forwards."

As I look back, I find it particularly fascinating that, working closely with Tres Pestalozzi and Dominik Wlodarczak, I had the privilege of experiencing the early nineteen-nineties on the spot: the abrupt and globally significant political transition of Russia from seventy years of a communist and totalitarian Soviet empire to an unregulated capitalist model (early capitalism). These were truly the foundation years of the new Russia, the Wild East! This shocking and rapid change was coupled with enormous financial and existentially threatening sacrifices on the part of a large portion of the population who suffered impoverishment at the hands of the new order, while, at the same time, a small minority became extremely wealthy in a short period of time. This minority had achieved their success largely by exploiting the grey areas and dark spots of an economy undergoing transformation, particularly the weak governmental structures that no longer functioned, allowing corruption to flourish unabated.

But it must not be forgotten that as a consequence of the demise of the Soviet Union all citizens gained new freedoms and more responsibility. Although I have identified and described many defects of privatization, it is clear to me today that the reformers in 1991 were faced with the sheer impossibility of the task of leading the Soviet commando economy into a system based on supply and demand. As I have tried to illustrate with various personal experiences, in the early nineteen-nineties prices were set without regulation, property rights were established, and privatization was introduced for the first time. For the most part, the reformers attained these goals. Their greatest achievement has been the successful transition from a planned economy to a market economy, which today can no longer be reversed. Yet the resulting hardships for much of the population, especially for the older generation, were so great that in 1996, when Yeltsin was reelected, the communists almost regained the upper hand. Avoiding such a takeover was initially the most important goal of the reformers – and in the end they succeeded.

## Chapter 34

ACKNOWLEDGMENTS

In spring 2011, in Aarau, I happened to run into Dominik Wlodarzak, my one-time assistant from the time of the Russian campaign. It had been a long time since we had met, and we spoke a bit nostalgically of our unforgettable experiences at the time of the "turn" in Russia (1993–94). Neither of us had read anything about this period written by business people who had been there themselves. I told Dominik that I was prepared to write a book about this time as a witness, provided he would support me with his outstanding memory, if not actually participating in writing the book. Dominik agreed enthusiastically, while pointing out that while he had little time at his disposal to serve as a co-author, he would gladly serve in an unofficial capacity as a contributor. Thanks in part to his astute observations and that of others present in Russia during a critical time in her history, this book came into being, serving as a testimonial of events experienced by first-hand observers.

As the book progressed, Dominik and I got the idea of asking other "Russian warriors" of the time to contribute to the book. Thus I am indebted also to Cyrille Kisselevsky, Kurt Häfeli, Marc Wurtz, and Alexander Vogler for their lively descriptions of events that had unfolded during that dramatic period of Russia's history. Particular thanks are due also to the long-time Russian connoisseur, Dr. Karl Eckstein, who undertook some important additions and corrections.

The sometimes very lonely writer, the author of this book, was encouraged to continue writing by the positive feedback expressed by Felix Gähwiler, Dr. Paul Fink, and Dr. Max D. Amstutz, as well as by the former Swiss Ambassador Dr. Johann Bucher.

# The author

Derrick Widmer studied jurisprudence at the University of Bern, The University of Chicago Law School, the University of Mexico D.F., and business at the Harvard Business School. He is past director of the Swiss Holcim Cement Group Support, former president of a Swiss military court with the rank of colonel. Other credits include: founder and long-time president of the Swiss-Indian Chamber of Commerce, former Honorary Consul to the Republic of Kazakhstan, former President of the 18 Swiss Schools Abroad (educationsuisse), President of the Argovia Philharmonic Orchestra, and Vice-president of the Swiss-Russian Forum. Additionally, he served on the board of two foundations dedicated to raising scholarships for talented youth from under-privileged backgrounds.

His publishing credits include: 1) America in the Early 1960's – A Love Story; 2) The Merry Mad Monks of the DMC: Memories of an Adventurous Life on the Thirty Eighth Parallel in Korea (an autobiographical novel, 1964); 3) Kunst in Holderbank (twenty expositions of contemporary art, published more recently than his other books).

**novum** 🔖 PUBLISHER FOR NEW AUTHORS

# The publisher

*He who stops
getting better
stops being good.*

This is the motto of novum publishing, and our focus is on finding new manuscripts, publishing them and offering long-term support to the authors.
Our publishing house was founded in 1997, and since then it has become THE expert for new authors and has won numerous awards.

**Our editorial team will peruse each manuscript within a few weeks free of charge and without obligation.**

You will find more information about
novum publishing and our books on the internet:

w w w . n o v u m p u b l i s h i n g . c o m

# Rate this book on our website!

www.novumpublishing.com